Praise for Hannah Alexander

"The rapport of Alexander's characters is both realistic and engaging in this tautly thrilling tale."
—*RT Book Reviews* on *Eye of the Storm*

"With its suspense, danger, characters and other strong elements, Hannah Alexander's *Hidden Motive* is an excellent story that's sure to keep you up late."
—*RT Book Reviews*

Praise for Jill Elizabeth Nelson

"This book has a well-developed plot and an excellent mystery that will keep you guessing until the final pages."
—*RT Book Reviews* on *Legacy of Lies*

"A wonderful mystery with a great heroine keeps the reader guessing."
—*RT Book Reviews* on *Witness to Murder*

HANNAH ALEXANDER

is the pseudonym of husband-and-wife writing team Cheryl and Mel Hodde (pronounced "Hoddee"). When they first met, Mel had just begun his new job as an ER doctor in Cheryl's hometown, and Cheryl was working on a novel. Cheryl's matchmaking pastor set them up on an unexpected blind date at a local restaurant. Surprised by the sneak attack, Cheryl blurted the first thing that occurred to her: "You're a doctor? Could you help me paralyze someone?" Mel was shocked. "Only temporarily, of course," she explained when she saw his expression. "And only fictitiously. I'm writing a novel."

They began brainstorming immediately. Eighteen months later they were married, and the novels they set in fictitious Ozark towns began to sell. The first novel in the Hideaway series won the prestigious Christy Award for Best Romance in 2004.

JILL ELIZABETH NELSON

writes what she likes to read—faith-based tales of adventure seasoned with romance. By day she operates as housing manager for a seniors' apartment complex. By night she turns into a wild and crazy writer who can hardly wait to jot down all the exciting things her characters are telling her, so she can share them with her readers. More about Jill and her books can be found at jillelizabethnelson.com. She and her husband live in rural Minnesota, surrounded by the woods and prairie and their four grown children, who have settled nearby.

COUNTDOWN TO DANGER

HANNAH ALEXANDER
JILL ELIZABETH NELSON

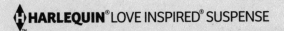

HARLEQUIN® LOVE INSPIRED® SUSPENSE

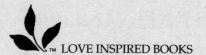

™ LOVE INSPIRED BOOKS

ISBN-13: 978-0-373-67653-8

Countdown to Danger

Copyright © 2015 by Harlequin Books S.A.

The publisher acknowledges the copyright holders of the individual works as follows:

Alive After New Year
Copyright © 2015 by Hannah Alexander

New Year's Target
Copyright © 2015 by Jill Elizabeth Nelson

Recycling programs for this product may not exist in your area.

www.Harlequin.com

Printed in U.S.A.

CONTENTS

ALIVE AFTER NEW YEAR

HANNAH ALEXANDER

This book is dedicated to the caretakers
of Jolly Mill Park and to the founders long ago
in history who built it into a thriving community
for those traveling by wagon train.

ALIVE AFTER NEW YEAR

Hannah Alexander

This book is dedicated to the caretakers
of Jolly Mill Park and to the founders long ago
in history who built it into a thriving community
for those traveling by wagon train.

Finally, brothers, whatever is true, whatever is right, whatever is pure, whatever is lovely, whatever is admirable—if anything is excellent or praiseworthy, think about such things.

—*Philippians* 4:8

ONE

Too stunned to move, Lynley Marshall pressed numb fingers against the sliding glass door that led out onto the lower deck of her mom's house. A lurid red note pasted eye level outside on the glass glared at her with a green, jagged font and accusing words. The Christmas colors had drawn her to the note initially. Now its writer had ruined Christmas for her forever. She didn't dare open the door to retrieve it until she knew whether or not someone might be out there waiting.

K.M: Your precious daughter is a killer and deserves to die. Wire me four million dollars before December 31 or she won't live to see New Year's Day. You gave birth to her, you will pay. Be alone and ready for my instructions in six days. Don't contact authorities unless you wish to lose her sooner.

Lynley sucked in a hard breath. KM? That meant Kirstie Marshall. Mom. This note was to Mom? Rereading the note, she felt the numbness in her fingers spread up her hands. She backed away from the door and into the shadows, where the few patches of morning sun that reached the lower deck couldn't reveal her to whoever might be watching. Someone wanted to kidnap her?

Nothing moved out in the gray and cedar-green forest past the deck railing that overlooked the se-cluded village of Jolly Mill. Even the tiniest of tree branches seemed frozen in clear amber. The only movement she sensed was the skin on her arms as it tightened into gooseflesh. She could see no footprints on the decking to suggest that someone had recently been here, but that meant nothing since she'd swept snow from the deck yesterday.

Someone must want retribution. Lynley could guess why. But to get it from Mom?

She paced from the kitchen to the living room, shaking with fear and fury.

Lynley had known from the first notice of the malpractice suit three years ago that the family of a patient who died under her nursing care was after money. It didn't matter to them that no one could have saved their drugged daughter, or that her overdose was her choice, not Lynley's, even though she'd been the nurse in charge of triage the night the patient came in. There was no way of knowing that this had been the one time Wendy Freeson had gone too far.

Hospitals had deep pockets, so the family had attempted to squeeze money from her employer through the court system. Since the court had ruled against the plaintiff, could the plaintiff be looking for another way to get to her?

It infuriated Lynley that someone was vindictive and greedy enough to threaten her—and her mother! Via television, radio and the printed word, news had spread throughout the region about her uncle Lawson's death and Mom's inheritance.

Lynley's respiratory rate, along with her heart rate, increased. Her insides trembled. Someone had gone to the trouble to find out where Mom lived—to discover, even, where Mom typically preferred to sit and greet the dawn with a cup of espresso. Today, however, she'd had no time because of an early meeting.

Oh, yes, someone knew about those millions, but they obviously didn't know enough. So who erroneously believed Mom was now wealthy? Not a Jolly Mill citizen. They all knew better.

The smell of Lynley's coffee lingered in the kitchen, but it mingled with anxiety to make her stomach queasy. Mom would have gone straight to the garage this morning, and she'd missed this tasteless piece of paper, but what about next time? She had to be warned.

Lynley closed her eyes and gritted her teeth, fighting back a bitter terror. The note writer could be on the upper deck this very minute. The house had double decks leading from the kitchen and dining room, as well as the upper guest room. Both had sliding glass doors and upper windows that allowed anyone a good view into the house from the right angle, though no one could see into the house from the front. She'd always appreciated that openness to the morning light. Until now.

From inside, she could see the bottom of the upper deck. She glanced up between the slats of the wooden floor that had tripped her so many times when she was a child. She could see no movement, only those evenly spaced rows of light, enriched by the morning sun that cast shadows of crisscrossed lines on the lower deck.

She was reaching to unlock the door to slide it open and grab the note when the doorbell rang. She jerked around and stared at the solid oak door thirty feet away. Who could that be? Mom wouldn't ring the doorbell.

Something brushed against her leg. Lynley shrieked and looked down to find Data, one of Mom's cats, on his usual affectionate marking journey through the house.

She heard rushing footsteps alongside the house and up the short stairway that led to the bottom deck. She searched the kitchen cabinet for a weapon…any weapon.

The edge of a shadow reflected against the glass door and she scrambled aside, screaming again as she drew a handle haphazardly from the wooden knife block. She turned, holding it in front of her. It was a butcher knife, sharp and heavy. She could have been holding a toothpick and she'd have felt as safe.

But then Police Chief John Russell stepped into view, weapon drawn, face grim. She released a breath and slumped with relief against the counter. He froze when he saw the knife, and then his gaze went to her face, which must have certainly shown her fear.

Without intending to, she glanced once more at the object of that fear, and John followed the line of her sight. He looked to the note, which was taped on the outside of the door. He reached for it, of course unable to read it from his vantage point.

"No. John, oh, no!" She lunged forward, still holding the knife. What if someone was watching? What if the person knew he was the policeman in this town?

He stopped midreach and stared at her through the glass, lowering his hand. "Lynley?" The thick double pane muted his voice. "What's wrong? I was just bringing some of your favorite blueberry muffins and I heard you cry out. Is someone in there? Are you in trouble?" Once again he reached for the red square of paper, weapon still drawn.

"Don't touch the note!" She set her knife on the kitchen counter and flipped open the lock on the door.

He rolled the heavy glass backward and stepped inside. "Lynley? What's wrong?" He peered around the living area and kitchen, as if seeking an intruder.

"I...I'm just a little, uh, creeped out." She couldn't keep her gaze from skimming the note again, like a rabbit staring at a rattler. How could she distract John from it?

Of course, that was when he decided to turn and look at it. "What on earth is going on?" He paused, and she could feel his body stiffen.

"John, please. Someone could be watching, and they warned—"

He holstered his weapon. "KM? This is to your mother?" He reached back out the door and lifted the note from the glass. "What kind of sick joke—"

"It doesn't look like a joke to me."

"Yeah, but someone's asking for millions of—"

"Mom's uncle Lawson had money. He died of cancer before you came to town, and Mom and her brother were the only heirs. All the wild speculations died down before you arrived and the rumor mill moved on to other things."

"You never told me this."

"Nothing to tell. Mom's portion of the inheritance went to help support the homeless rehab center at her request."

He held the note up. "We're looking at attempted extortion here."

Lynley picked up the butcher knife and slid it back into its slot in the block. She turned and studied the forest outside, searching for movement. "The media made a huge deal about my mom's inheritance near the beginning of the malpractice trial."

"Then this note is meant to sound as if it's written by the plaintiff."

Lynley turned back to him. "What do you mean 'meant to'?"

"Money makes people crazy, especially when it runs into the millions of dollars. Leave it to the media to blast that kind of half-baked information to the public for anyone to know."

The media had also basically used a manure spreader to broadcast all the tidbits they could dig up about her father. She'd never told John about him, either. It wasn't something a woman was quick to tell a man on a first date...or a second or third, so it had become too easy to avoid the subject. Why share the humiliation of being the child of a sociopath?

"It's nice to know you didn't go digging into

my past online to find out what you could about me," she murmured.

He gave her a brief, warm smile before returning his attention to the note. "Why spoil the fun of making friends the old-fashioned way?"

Friends. Yes. They were buddies who had made it clear without really saying so that a nice, solid friendship was exactly what they wanted. Right now, however, she could use the comfort of a strong shoulder to support her. She looked up into John's gentle gaze and felt herself leaning forward. He reached for her almost hesitantly, and she closed her eyes and stepped forward, allowing her forehead to press against his chest as he wrapped his arms around her.

This didn't happen often. She seldom admitted to weakness, seldom allowed herself to get this close to John, even after five months of friendship and trips to the lake, the movies, town activities.

There was something about a man who didn't push himself on her. John had his own walls, and that was just fine with her. Still, his arms felt good, and he was a much-needed port in this new, frightening storm.

John studied the interior of the house as he held Lynley's trembling body in his arms. Something about her vulnerability brought out a double dose of his protective instincts.

He glanced back outside, and realized this wasn't a wise position to be in. He stiffened and drew her into the shadows of the house, then gave her a tight hug before stepping away from her. He couldn't be distracted by a very attractive woman in need of comfort when he should keep his mind on possible dangers nearby.

"Is the house locked?" he asked, fingering the .40 mm Glock in his holster.

"Mom keeps most doors and windows double-locked, especially after our recent rash of scares."

"Good. We need to figure out who left this note and why, obviously," he said.

"You don't think it's from someone in Wendy Freeson's family out for revenge, because the court decision didn't go their way?"

"The trial isn't directly mentioned at all."

"Of course not. It isn't as if they'd paint a target for you to find."

"We'll check out the plaintiffs, of course, but since the trial is now a matter of public record, anyone could find this and decide to hold it over your head—*if* they believe there's money to be extorted, thanks to the great work of the mighty media." He was acquainted with a few photojournalists who managed to maintain their integrity and their jobs, but very few.

Lynley closed her eyes. He'd never seen her so terrified. In the months he'd known her, he'd seldom seen this side of her. He felt a surge of tenderness. It was an emotion he'd battled more and more the longer he knew her.

"What monster would do this to Mom? And to me?" She rubbed her forehead, as if an answer might come out if she pressed hard enough. "Too much has happened in Jolly Mill. It's like someone, some…thing…has us in its sights and plans to destroy us one way or—"

"Lynley, it's going to be okay." Perhaps this powerful urge he felt to grab her and never let her go came from a need to comfort himself, as well. Lynley was in someone's crosshairs, and he had to stop it. "You know, don't you, that any crank with half a brain will warn his victim not to contact the police? Besides, this note is to your mother, not you, so if you look at it that way, the rules don't apply. She didn't show the note to anyone. I found it."

She scowled at the note. "I don't think this person's playing by any list of rules." With a shake of her head, she paced away from him, into the darkness of the unlit living room and as far as possible from the deck. "Maybe I'll have a chance to show them my own set of rules. Don't mess with the Marshalls."

He grinned at the fierceness she showed despite her fear. He'd married the last woman he'd known with that much courage. But what had Sandra's courage earned her? A long, hard-fought battle against cancer that ravaged her body and finally won.

"Few people have the ability to follow through on their threats," he assured Lynley. "In the first place, they seldom have a way to even know you've called anyone, much less the police. I guess we can be glad Jolly Mill couldn't afford to buy a car for their only police officer, if someone really is watching the house somehow." He held his arms out to display a long-sleeve dark gray flannel shirt that went with his regular jeans. "No one can tell I'm driving a police car and I'm not wearing a uniform. No one knows I'm a cop unless they know me, even if they're looking at us from the forest right now."

"You don't think the note's from someone in the Freeson family, then?" Her voice suddenly sounded so tired, so vulnerable.

John wanted to pull her close again and tell her everything would be okay. But he knew too much about the world. "I only got in on the end of the trial since moving here. I don't think the Freeson relatives ever shared an authentic tear over Wendy's death. From all accounts I found, they didn't know her. But any family member can bring a lawsuit for a wrongful death, no matter how ridiculous."

"That I believe," she said. "I wasn't surprised to

learn they'd had to hunt down an attorney all the way down in Florida—some guy with a license to practice in Missouri—because they couldn't find anyone nearby to take their case."

"The guys in the precinct back in Sikeston used to joke that half of the attorneys in practice graduated in the lower fifty percent of their classes."

Finally, she gave a grim smile. "The attorney who took the Freeson case must have had a particularly low graduating score."

He nodded, glad to hear another surge of fight in her voice.

"Wendy's medical record showed she was what the emergency department personnel called a frequent flier," she said. "She cried wolf too often. How could I have known that one time, out of the dozens of times she showed up demanding narcotics for make-believe pain, that she'd overdose?"

John heard the grim tone of Lynley's compassion, despite the fact that Wendy had caused her own death by the illegal use of someone else's buffet of prescription medications.

The only person he'd known to shed a tear about Wendy's death was Lynley Marshall, the triage nurse who'd been unfairly blamed for it.

Lynley walked into the kitchen for a drink of water, glancing with obvious trepidation toward the woods past the deck.

Now was not the time, of course, but John

couldn't keep from admiring the grace of her movements, the beauty of her slender, athletic form. Her lush, thick, dark brown hair fell across her face as she leaned forward, covering the firm chin and graceful lines of her face.

She walked back into the shadows of the living room, shoulders hunched, looking miserable. She was obviously held in the grip of a shock so profound that she looked to him for direction. This was not like her at all.

Time to start the investigation process. He walked past her and touched her shoulder, squeezed it. For a moment she appeared to be leaning toward him.

"That lawsuit's been a nightmare from beginning to end," she whispered. "Now it seems there's actually not going to be an end."

"I did some background checking on the Freesons after I got here."

She blinked up at him. "You never told me that."

"I didn't want to distract you."

"What did you find out?"

"None of the family members had a history of violence, no prison records, nothing. I wouldn't expect any of them to be rocket scientists, but Wendy was the only problem family member. As you already know, they were distant cousins."

"If only I'd paid closer attention to her when I did triage that night, but her vitals were stable, and she looked the same way she'd looked the three times I'd seen her before during that same week. How could I have known she was in trouble on that particular night? She'd refused the CT scan and left against medical advice."

"Which cleared you." He waited until she looked up and met his gaze. "You're second-guessing yourself again. You did everything right, and the court decision bore that out."

She closed her eyes. "I know." She looked back up at him. "But what you're saying is that anyone could be behind this…this perverse joke." She jabbed her fingers at the Christmas-colored note. "Everyone in the 417 area code knew about Lawson's death and the inheritance."

"Everyone but me, apparently. It's almost as if this little macabre greeting card came from someone using public records as a fulcrum. The demand is for money, not revenge."

"But so was the lawsuit." Lynley caught her breath. "Mom. She could be in danger." She rushed back to the phone beside the sofa. "I need to get her back here."

John pulled out his cell and spoke Gerard Vance's name. In seconds he was talking to the only other man in Jolly Mill with good police experience—Vance was a former cop from Corpus Christi, Texas, who'd given up his career to use family money and help the homeless. Another set of eyes on this situation would be helpful right now, and Kirstie was at the rehab center today.

The former cop's deep voice greeted him in the middle of the first ring. "Hey, Chief. You change your mind about helping in the kitchen today?"

"Sorry. As a matter of fact, I need to see you. Now, please. I'm at Kirstie's with Lynley. Could you bring her down with you?"

"Hey, this sounds serious. What's up?"

"Her daughter's life has just been threatened."

"Lynley!"

"Bring protection."

"Let me hunt down Kirstie and I'll get her there."

John disconnected and nodded to Lynley. "I'm here, and I won't let anything happen to you."

TWO

Though Lynley knew John meant every word, she still wished she could return to a few moments ago, when she felt safe in his arms. She resisted the urge to move closer to him. After her disaster of a marriage, she vowed to never again place herself in such a vulnerable position. When she made that vow, however, she hadn't counted on befriending a man like John, who had all the characteristics her ex-husband had lacked.

"And what of you?" she asked.

His eyebrows raised in surprise. "What about me?"

"While you're placing yourself in harm's way to protect me, who's going to protect you?" When they'd first begun seeing each other on a friendly basis, she'd promised herself that she would break off the friendship if it threatened to turn into something more. Of course, when she first felt the threat looming in her heart, she'd struggled to convince herself she could certainly control her own emotions, and that breaking off their friendship would be a mistake.

She'd lied to herself, of course. Right now she could no more control her feelings toward John than she could scout out the person who threatened her life. The thought of John incurring injury in his duty to protect her was like a kick in the gut.

She should have read the signs months ago—about the time she found herself driving here to Mom's when she had more than one day off at a time. Her apartment in Springfield had become oppressive lately. Lonely. She studied John's face and realized it had become more precious to her every time she saw him—which was every time she came home.

John, too, appeared to look forward to her days off.

He tapped her on the arm. "This town is a safe place to be. You can stop worrying."

"Yes, but—"

"Have you seen Gerard or his lovely wife on the shooting range recently?"

John's mention of her best friend from childhood was intended to distract her, and it worked to a point. She grinned. "You know, I'm not bad, myself. Megan's been working with me on my aim. But neither Gerard, Megan nor I are paid to place ourselves in harm's way. You are."

His light green eyes seemed to dance with

humor, though she suspected it was a little forced. He leaned a couple of inches into her personal space. "Why, Lynley Marshall, I do believe you're actually worried about my safety."

She couldn't help it, the man's voice, his scent, even his body language made her want him closer. And that made her uncomfortable, and she felt it settle into her expression.

He backed off, and she couldn't miss a twitch of his lips, a creasing beside his eyes, as if he could read her and was suppressing yet another teasing retort. Why did he confuse her so?

"Forgive me," he said, his voice suddenly gentle. "I'm being a typical man. We like to beat our chests and rumble like apes, but some of us truly appreciate the caring tenderness of a woman concerned for our safety."

To her surprise, it seemed that his eyes said, "Especially this woman." But of course, she'd been intentionally alone for so long she wasn't in the habit of reading a man's mind.

Did he realize how fear completely controlled her? She feared for the friendship that had begun between them so easily. Somewhere the lines blurred, and the energy between them caught fire like a barn ablaze, and that fire threatened the safety of their comfortable friendship. Even if that weren't the case, however, she would still fear for his safety, especially considering the surprising dangers that had erupted in Jolly Mill these past years.

"You're not a typical man, John," she said softly. "Not at all."

And then it was her turn to suppress a smile when he blinked, lips parted. Though he didn't move away from her, something about him withdrew ever so subtly.

That had been their unspoken dance lately. Move forward, step back, keep time with music they couldn't actually hear, but that controlled them much more than either of them would have liked.

She knew about John's obvious unwillingness to reconnect after the great loss he'd experienced when his wife died. His cousin Emma had told Lynley all about it. A man like him didn't recover from a true love like that as quickly as people expected him to. It only drew her to him more profoundly.

But she needed John now, and she needed this dance of romance to not get in the way. They both needed their wits about them.

John touched the tip of her nose with his finger and grinned into her eyes with such warmth and acceptance, she felt reassured.

"I know how to protect myself, Lynley. A fella doesn't last long as a policeman if he can't do that."

Breathing as deeply and deliberately as she

could, she nodded. She felt like a needy woman who couldn't function without a man, and that was one thing she'd fought against since she walked in on her father and one of his many lady friends when she was a young teen. That day she'd vowed that this was the one path of her mother's that she didn't want to follow.

And then she vowed it again after her divorce from the man who turned out just like Daddy.

John got up and reached for the knife she'd held earlier and placed it into her hand. He locked the deck door. "Stay here. I'll be right back."

Data wandered back toward Lynley and trilled at her, his serious golden eyes staring into hers as if he knew. Yes, as Dean Koontz had once pointed out in a novel, cats knew things. Data knew more than most, and he had an extensive language that she wished she could understand. He howled when she cried, and she could tell from the tone of his trill that he was worried about her.

John checked the rest of the house with weapon in hand. Lynley sank into the love seat. Data jumped onto her lap. He nudged her chin with his cold, wet nose and his purr gave her a tiny sense of normalcy in this otherwise treacherous morning—as she believed it was meant to.

She buried her face in a white splotch of his black-and-white fur, and came up with a nose filled with cat hair. "Oh, Data, I love you dearly, but right now I wish God had placed you into the body of a Rottweiler."

But people also killed big, scary animals to get to their victims. Who knew what a crazy person would do?

John returned with his weapon holstered once more. "I'll call the hospital, let them know what's happening."

"Why?"

"To cancel your shifts for the rest of the week."

"No. We get some tough characters in the ER, and we have tough men who can handle them. Our guys work out."

His eyes narrowed just a tad. Was that a hint of jealousy she saw there? "So do I." His voice was almost too quiet. "But why risk an unnecessary attack?"

"Finding another nurse to cover for me—"

"Can be done more easily than hiring extra security to protect you and everyone around you."

She didn't feel like arguing. "Where's Mom? Isn't she supposed to be here by now?"

John hesitated and glanced at his watch. "Gerard would have called if there was a problem." But he didn't sound as sure as she'd have liked.

She knew she wouldn't be able to breathe deeply until Mom came walking through the front door, safe and secure.

Christmas celebrations had just come to a nasty

stop, and Lynley had no idea what the New Year would bring for Jolly Mill, Missouri.

John watched Lynley with the practiced eye of his profession. It was a good thing he'd learned the hard lessons on the police force: things about keeping his frightened thoughts to himself, keeping his emotions from showing on his face—most of the time—and keeping a steady hand on his weapon. Controlling his behavior didn't help with his usual gut response to stress, but knowing he could be fit and ready to face what came at him did help him feel safer. Not cocky, just competent.

He stepped out to the glass doors once more to study what he could of the forest to the east of the house. Still no movement. Unfortunately, no one else lived to the east of the house, but someone from the village below, across the creek, might have seen someone here earlier. This afternoon he or Gerard could make some calls, and he was sure Kirstie would want to contact her friends.

He thanked God for Gerard Vance, ex-cop, guardian of those in need. The big man had about twenty pounds on John—mostly muscle—and a couple of years on him, as well, which helped in situations that required experience. John hadn't realized, when he moved here and took this job in the summer, how difficult it would be to handle the job without backup. He missed his colleagues in Sikeston.

John glanced over his shoulder to the love seat, where Lynley allowed Data, Kirstie's black-and-white ten-ton cat, to maul her into a furry mess. Focusing on everyday things gave him peace. Apparently, it comforted Lynley, as well, because she simply brushed the fur from her face and continued to snuggle. The cat actually had his front legs wrapped around Lynley's neck. John could hear a loud purr from where he stood.

It had been over ten minutes since John called Gerard. Like Lynley, he'd expected to see them here five minutes ago. The homeless rehab center was within walking distance from here—barely a block and a half uphill.

He left Lynley cuddling the cat and took the stairs to the upper hallway, where he could get a better perspective of the hillside to the east. Something caught his attention—movement below, near the creek, too far away to get a good look, or even to tell if it was male or female, only that the figure was an adult.

Before he could turn to hunt down Kirstie's binoculars to get a better look at the figure, several people came running out of the center up on the hillside above the house, and he saw a child tripping around the winter leaves, far above the mystery person.

He called Gerard once more, feeling overly dependent as he did so.

"Sorry, John," Gerard said when he answered. "We had us a little emergency." There were chattering voices, a crying child, shouting in the background.

"Let me guess. A child hunt?"

"You've been watching. Yep, one of the little ones wandered outside, and his parents couldn't find him for a few minutes. He's probably not going to do that again. Gave us a fright, though, especially me, in light of your own little scare."

For a moment, John pondered that. "Got a question for you, but don't take offense." With as few words as possible, John filled Gerard in on the situation, then said, "You don't think anyone from your center could—"

"You're wondering if your culprit might be someone from here."

"It crossed my mind. I'm looking for any and all answers at this point."

"I've considered it. I'm not omniscient, John. No matter how many background checks I give these people before we bring them here, it's always possible someone could slip through. When I convinced the town council to let us set up shop here, I gave my word that no harm would come to the town because of it. I'll do anything to keep that promise."

"That child wouldn't have chanced to spot someone else in the woods, do you think?"

"Why? Did you see someone else?"

"Sure did."

"Hold on, let me ask."

John waited while he heard a conflagration of voices in the background. Most of the homeless people who came to the rehab center were city folk, and they didn't realize that the woods in Missouri were much safer than most city streets.

Gerard spoke again. "Poor kid was lost and was looking for our building. He wasn't paying attention."

"Out of curiosity, am I the only person in Jolly Mill who didn't know about the inheritance until Lynley told me a few minutes ago?"

"Probably, but that's not surprising." The noise in the background suddenly disappeared, and a door shut. Gerard had stepped outside. "Here in our town, most folks still see honor in police authority, so gossiping to you would be kind of like gossiping to a preacher. They'd be ashamed. But sharing tantalizing information with the folks here at the center just means they're being accepted by some of the townsfolk. Kind of encouraging, actually."

"So you're saying everyone up at the center knew about Kirstie's supposed inheritance."

"I know some of them do, some of those who've

been around longer, but they also know that her money was given to us to help them, and she's treated like a queen around here. That's one reason I don't think we need to worry about our people."

"Unless some of them believe she still has money. Before you come down, would you have your staff start asking the residents if any of them saw someone outside Kirstie's house earlier this morning?"

"You don't want to keep this thing quiet, then."

"At first I thought it would be a good idea, but something I said to Lynley got me to thinking. We're going to have to ask questions, anyway, and you know word's going to spread quickly. Why not use that to our advantage?"

"You're a good man, John Russell. I don't care what everyone else says about you."

John rolled his eyes. "Thanks. You're a real pal."

"We can't keep a sneeze secret around here, anyway, so why not put all that extra hot air to good use?"

"Is Kirstie with you now?"

"She's just inside, helping corral the others and putting some finishing touches on food prep."

"Does she know her daughter needs her?"

"Not yet. We'll be down as soon as I task Megan with the questioning."

"Then let me warn you, Lynley intends to work her two shifts at the hospital this week."

Gerard grunted. "Not good."

"Where are you now?"

"I'm getting ready to grab Kirstie and get her home."

John waited and listened as Gerard Vance reentered a noisy room—the kitchen, from the sound of it, the talk and chatter of rehab residents—and heard Vance's soothing voice as he asked Kirstie to follow him. To her credit, she didn't ask a single question.

"You got it, boss. I don't like battering chicken, anyway. Just let me wash my hands."

John couldn't help smiling when he heard Kirstie Marshall's voice in the background. Lynley's mother had the light laughter of a happy teen, and though her life had been filled with hard knocks, she looked forward to the future, and seldom grieved the past.

"She's washing up," Vance told John. "We'll be there in five unless another child wanders off."

"You're parked in the garage?"

"Sure. Don't worry, I'll get her into the truck without going outside, and I'll lock the doors. This one's got you worried, my friend."

"And Lynley."

"Yep." Vance cleared his throat. "You do know how…um…strong-willed Lynley is."

"I've had time to figure that out."

"You can't let her run this investigation."

"No, and I'll do what it takes to keep her from working those shifts this week. They're back-to-back, and so she'd be staying in her apartment in Springfield to avoid the hour-long drive each way."

"Not good. Do what you can."

John powered off and glanced around the deck, then peered into the forest to the east of the house. No one lingered down below now. As Lynley said, someone could be watching from anywhere, but he didn't get the feeling of being watched. Not that he was going to place Lynley's safety into the fettered hands of emotion.

He heard a soft rumble, and realized Lynley had slid open the glass door below him. Data darted outside, his bright white-and-black coat likely drawing the attention of endangered squirrels, birds and mice anywhere within a quarter-mile radius, since it was an unseasonably warm day. Lynley's urgent call to the playful cat went unheeded.

That cat was the darling of Kirstie's life, next in line to Lynley, of course. No one took Lynley's place. John could see why. Despite his initial resistance to a growing friendship with a living, breathing woman, Lynley's calm determination and gentle spirit had wrapped themselves around him from the first time he met her, and he'd been unable get her image out of his mind when he closed his eyes at night. She was first in his thoughts when he woke up the next morning.

Though he was firm in his determination to remain single, this threat against her life both enraged and stunned him with the depth of caring he'd developed for her in these past months. It wasn't what he'd intended. He'd moved here to be close to his cousins—plus the challenge of being the police chief and only policeman in a town of eight hundred had been difficult to refuse.

He saw Data climb to the upper deck and sniff around the railing—as if he picked up an unusual scent, perhaps? John tapped the window. The strikingly beautiful cat stood outside the glass, and his gold-foil eyes, white face and pink nose with a black splotch on his head made John smile. He'd never been a cat person, but these cats of Kirstie's had shown him anything could happen.

He stepped into Kirstie's library, where she kept a list of birds she'd seen in the area. Beside the list were her binoculars. He took them back with him to the door and studied the woods, from the rehab center to the creek and beyond. No figure was in sight.

Sliding open the upper deck door to lure Data back inside, he watched for Vance's truck to come around the curve above the house. As soon as the cat darted in, John shut and locked the door, eager to get back downstairs to reassure Lynley that

Data was fine. What was it about having friends in physical proximity that made one feel all would be well?

He knew better. If he let down his guard, no one would be safe. He followed Data to the stairway and saw Lynley coming up, her dark brown eyes filled with relief when she saw Data.

"You little scamp. You just did that to show me you could." She flipped his jauntily curling tail as he raced past her, then gave John a smile. "Thanks. I don't want Mom worrying about two of us at the same time."

John swallowed hard. He had a job to do, and he couldn't be distracted by a sweet smile or a deep gaze from dark brown eyes. How long had he been lying to himself about her, trying to convince himself they were good friends. Buddies. Nothing more?

This was the moment he must see himself as nothing but her protector.

Sandra would likely be cheering right now if she knew he'd begun to feel a shift in his mindset, but he was not cheering. Something about losing a wife to death left a man feeling married and wanting to be faithful. Yes, it also left him lonely, and he knew that wasn't what she wanted. In fact, he'd expected to recover from his loss long before now. It wasn't until the fourth year after her death that he realized there would be no recovery. Life would continue whether he wanted it to or not, but he'd lost a vital part of himself when Sandra died, and contrary to what everyone had tried to tell him, time was no healer.

He just couldn't move forward. Not now. Maybe not ever.

THREE

Lynley met John halfway up the wide staircase and felt her body lean in his direction as if her mind and body were somehow disconnected. She refused to respond to the attraction she felt. Right now she was depending on him for her very life, so of course she wanted to hold on to him. Anything to connect to. Right?

He placed an arm around her, but didn't draw her close, as if he knew where her limits were, and had put on his professional persona. How instinctive this man was. Not pushy. Not overtly affectionate, even though she had no doubt he cared about her. What was it about him that could translate his thoughts and intentions to her without his having to say a word?

"This time Gerard really is on his way down with Kirstie. I saw someone downhill near the creek a moment ago," he said. "By the time I reached the binoculars, whoever it was had disappeared, but I'm suspicious. And something else about the note doesn't ring true."

She turned and looked up at him. "True in what way? I've been rereading it, studying every word, but I've read it so much the words are bleeding together."

"I want to show it to Gerard when he gets here with your mother, then we can talk about it. They were delayed by a missing child. He's been found."

She felt a jolt of fear. "How long was this child missing? John, what if the person who left this note had seen—"

"No, he wasn't gone for long."

"But there are so many children up there so close to us. What if they're in danger, too?"

He placed a calming hand on her shoulder. "Want me to make you a cup of chamomile tea?"

"No time. I'll take a GABA. I think Mom has some L-theanine in her stash of supplements." She felt so out of control, and she couldn't afford that right now. She sighed, dreading the moment Mom entered the house. "Does she know?"

"Not yet. When we tell her, I want her to start spreading the word around town. Megan's going to question everyone who might've seen anyone on the decks this morning."

Lynley's breath tumbled out. "You're taking this to the public? But John, the note said—"

"We aren't going to allow anyone near enough to you. That letter writer will not touch you." His green eyes filled with regret. "I'm sorry, Lynley. I can imagine how frightening this is—"

The thump of a car door startled her. Another followed. An injection of adrenaline shot through her arteries and tingled along her arms and hands. There was no more time to give in to fear. She hurried to the door just as her mother unlocked it and pushed it open.

Lynley fell into her arms, unable to hold back the trembling that set itself up deep inside her. This was a living nightmare.

"Sweetheart?" Mom drew her close, her whole body tensing within Lynley's grasp. "What is it?"

"Mom, some idiot stuck a ransom note for me on the back door."

Kirstie jerked away. "What!"

Gerard and John guided the two of them toward the cluster of sofa and recliners, and Lynley heard the door lock behind them. It wasn't until John pressed a tissue into her hand that she realized she was crying, and for a moment the tears were so abundant she could barely make out his face. This wasn't how she'd intended to behave.

Mom looked up at John, then Gerard. "What on earth?"

"We're checking into it," John said.

Lynley wiped her face, blew her nose, accepted

another tissue from John, furious with herself for behaving like a weak-kneed little girl.

"Why don't we sit down?" John drew Lynley forward, sharing a meaningful look with Gerard that Lynley couldn't miss.

They'd obviously already put some plans into place.

Lynley sank into the sofa cushions between John and Mom. John touched her shoulder, then reached for the note on the side table. Gerard perched on the sofa arm beside Kirstie.

As if to cushion the impact of the words, John read the note aloud, his voice soft and mellifluous.

"Who did this?" Kirstie growled loudly enough to make Data jump.

Lynley blinked. Sweet Kirstie Marshall became Mama Bear right there in front of everyone. Her eyes darkened like stormy skies beneath lowering brows. Lynley had seen it often, and though she'd been walking in terror since finding the note, she felt Mom's strength reach out and engulf her.

John studied mother and daughter with admiration. Lynley had been touched by God's grace when He gave her Kirstie Marshall for a mother. Though Lynley seldom spoke about her father, others had told him tidbits about Kirstie's late husband. Ugly man. Kirstie had the courage of a fighter along with a tender mother's touch.

Lynley had obviously inherited all her best traits from Kirstie.

"Someone's after your money, Kirstie." Gerard's deep voice rumbled through the spacious living room.

She looked up at him, eyes still dark and angry. "Barry seems to be stretching his big ol' greedy, bony hands from the grave. He always wanted Uncle Lawson's millions." She winced, then tapped her fingers to her lips and looked at Lynley. "Sweetheart, I'm sorry to speak ill of your father."

"You've always taught me to tell the truth. Why shouldn't you do the same?"

John caught Gerard's attention over the heads of the two women. "Your thoughts?"

"We can all agree that this note was written to imply that an angry plaintiff from the trial is still fighting for retribution," Gerard said.

John nodded, glad to know he and Gerard were thinking the same thing.

Kirstie's cell phone beeped its text chime. She ignored it. Lynley reached into her mother's purse, pulled out the phone and handed it to her.

Kirstie waved it away. "We have more important things to talk about right now."

"And someone knows where you live. They might know more."

With a sigh, Kirstie took the phone and punched

a button. Her eyes narrowed with renewed fury while she read. Her hand trembled.

Gerard took it from her. He read the text, then closed his eyes with a groan.

John grabbed the phone and looked at the text while Lynley read it aloud over his shoulder. "'You're a fool if you think I don't know what kind of car your chief of police drives. You just shortened your daughter's life. Get me the money before New Year's Eve or she will die. You're wasting time. Enjoy the muffins on your front porch. They'll be your daughter's last.'"

John had no clue about where the text had originated, but he could easily predict that if it were possible to call and have it tracked, it would have come from the woods to the east of the house—perhaps down closer to the creek. "Whoever wrote this was at the front of the house sometime after I arrived but before I brought in the muffins. They apparently haven't been watching all this time because they're writing to you, Kirstie."

"This is simply meant to frighten us," Gerard said. "We can't let that happen. Every resident in Jolly Mill knows the truth—that Lawson Barnes bequeathed everything to our center, and nothing ever went to Kirstie."

"So that can help us narrow down our suspects," John said. "Kirstie, why don't you start calling friends and bring them in on this? Spread the word. In a tiny place like Jolly Mill, the more eyes we have on strangers sneaking through town, the more likely we are to catch this—"

Kirstie nodded, her delicate chin jutting out with determination. "I'll call Nora first, of course, then Carmen."

John nodded. Kirstie Marshall was already planning. Her love for her daughter was one of her strongest assets.

Gerard frowned at the initial note. "This writer has been scanning information from the media. They were the ones who spread the lie far and wide that Lynley, a much-publicized defendant in the lawsuit, stood to inherit millions of dollars from a dead uncle." His lip curled in disgust. "Isn't it always about the money?"

"So we're all in agreement that we can rule out the plaintiffs in the malpractice trial." John looked at Lynley, then Gerard and Kirstie.

Gerard scrunched his flint-carved face. "We aren't working with absolutes right now. Not yet, anyway. I wouldn't rule it out, but their motive is greed. Somehow we need to convince this individual that there are no deep pockets for them to dig into."

John agreed. It was too soon to choose one direction to investigate. He'd seen bad results those times his colleagues made a judgment too early and let the real culprit get away.

Kirstie held the red-and-green note up by the tip of her thumb and finger, as if it might be contagious. "You're right. Someone knows that threatening my only child is the quickest way to get to me." She dropped the paper on the coffee table. "They don't know who they're dealing with, do they, sweetheart?" She nudged her daughter with her elbow.

Lynley nudged back. "Love you, too, Mom."

"Lynley," Gerard said, "we're not letting anybody near you."

"We can't rule out Jolly Mill and rehab center residents altogether," John said, "but I'm mostly working on the premise that this has to be someone from out of town."

Gerard's phone chimed, and he grabbed it and flipped it open. "Megan? You have news already, honey?"

John watched his friend's face as the charmed expression—the one he always wore when talking to his beloved wife—turned to stone once more.

"Blue car? What kind?" He listened some more, nodding as if his wife could see him. "Okay, hon. Thanks. That should help."

After he disconnected he turned to them, grim faced. "Mrs. Drews, who lives down by the Baptist church, was walking to work this morning when she saw a blue car park at the old Bethel Church on the road past the edge of town, so it was too far away to see what kind of car it was. Someone in a hoodie walked across the field toward the woods and went right through Capps Creek. Must've been wearing high waders."

"Then that's who I saw," John said.

"Could she tell if it was male or female?" Lynley asked.

"All we know is that someone's serious about this thing," John said. "We'd better start circling the wagons."

Lynley felt dizzy. She closed her eyes and rested her head on the back of the sofa.

A soft hand pressed against her arm. "Sweetheart, why don't you go lie down for a little bit." It was Mom's gentle voice.

Lynley opened her eyes and saw the three of them watching her with concern. She'd expect this kind of attention from her mother, but from two big, tough men with work to do and bad guys to catch? It scared her a little that they were so worried about her.

"The best way to keep Lynley safe is to find this person before New Year's Eve," John said. "And for Gerard or me to keep her with one of us at all times."

"Agreed," Mom said. "John, can you call in help? The sheriff?"

"I'm sorry, but one little note without a dead

body, they wouldn't give it a glance. Even in the winter months they're constantly fighting the drug trade."

"I'm wondering about one possibility." John glanced at Lynley as if braced for battle. "I'm thinking about someone who was once a member of the Marshall family, but no longer—"

"Dodge Knowles," Lynley said.

Mom stiffened beside her, and her hands clenched until her fingertips whitened. "I'd have thought Barry might have done something like this if he were still alive, but…"

"My father tried to kill you, Mom," Lynley said. "Who's to say I didn't choose the same kind of man?"

"Where is your ex-husband now, Lynley?" Gerard asked.

"I have no idea, but I doubt he's nearby," Lynley said. "I was so glad to see him out of my life I was willing to give up the house to the lazy lecher." She started to say more, but bit the tip of her tongue. It was something she'd never told Mom.

"But we never heard if he actually sold the house," Mom said. "And it's in Cassville. Barely a thirty-minute drive from here."

Lynley shook her head. "The only reason he wanted it was so he could sell it for the money. I sank every dime and spare moment I had into that place, and by the time it was finished it was worth twice what we paid for it. He was constantly talking about getting out of the state. He had a nursing license for Kansas, as well."

John jumped to his feet. "Mind if I use your computer, Kirstie? I'll check it out while y'all brainstorm other options."

Lynley sat in silence, recalling Dodge's multiple complaints when she'd insisted on leaving Kansas City and buying a place closer to Mom when she was battling breast cancer years ago. The one thing that had begun the destruction of their marriage was when he commented that if her mother died from cancer, at least he and Lynley would never have to work again. They'd be multimillionaires as soon as Kirstie's uncle died. It was on that day that Lynley discovered she'd married a man just like her dead father.

Lynley cast Mom a quick glance. She'd endured so much, but she was as filled with vitality as she ever had been. It gave Lynley a feeling of peace— the thought that maybe someday she'd be more like her mother, despite her late father's blood running through her veins. Mom was her rock.

The clatter of Kirstie's keyboard echoed through the house, and in the beams of sunlight coming through the windows, cat hair floated like stardust. If Mom had her way, this place would soon be crawling with friends, neighbors—most of them empowered with weapons and righteous indignation.

John returned to the room. "Found Dodge."

"Where?" Mom asked.

He gave Lynley a look of sympathy. "Apparently he's still living in the house he was awarded in the divorce settlement. He's in Cassville. He's working at the hospital in town."

Lynley slumped back into the sofa. "But I thought he was…gone."

"This makes him a candidate," John said. "He would have known about the family money. What he wouldn't know, since he's no longer connected to anyone in town, is that you don't have what he's after."

"There's another option," Gerard said. "We still have the bulk of Lawson's bequest in a special fund to support the center while we build the manufacturing plant at the edge of town."

Lynley sat up, horrified at what he would consider giving up. "Oh, no you don't. We are not giving the money to this fiend."

"It would be a way to buy time and track them down."

"Find another way," Lynley said. "That's not happening."

Mom touched her arm. "Honey, this is your life we're talking about."

"This is extortion. I refuse to let someone get

rich by using me as a pawn. We'll have to figure out something else."

"You can't tell me what to do with the money your mother donated to my cause," Gerard said gently.

Lynley paused to breathe, sorting through the streams of anger, terror and frustration that threatened to tie her in knots. "What if Dodge really is behind this?"

Mom met her gaze. "I never trusted that man, but I also never dreamed he would do something like this."

"We never dreamed my father would try to poison you with mercury, either," Lynley said.

Mom closed her eyes and shook her head. "It was always about the money for him, too."

Lynley's heart squeezed painfully at the sadness in her mother's voice. Mom had blamed herself for the choices her husband had made. It wasn't fair. He'd been the one to make those decisions, have those affairs, and even stoop so low as to poison her to get his hands on her uncle's money, and she took the blame for it? Not fair at all.

With a quick glance at John, Lynley reminded herself why she had no business even considering another man in her life. If her wise, insightful, mother couldn't read correctly into the heart of a man, what hope was there?

"My question, then," Gerard said, "is how much is Dodge like Barry?"

Lynley studied the lines of worry around Mom's eyes, the firm chin, the determined gaze.

"What do you think, sweetheart?" Mom asked. "Could that note have been from him?"

Lynley wanted to reach through the lines of that hideous note, the hateful text message to Mom, and discover where they originated. If only she had that kind of insight. But she didn't. "I think Dodge might be a place to start."

FOUR

Two days after Christmas, John was astounded to find himself driving Gerard's SUV down Highway 37 toward Cassville, Missouri, with Lynley Marshall, of all people, in the passenger seat. He'd had no choice, really. Gerard had an emergency with one of his rehab people this morning.

"I can't believe this," he muttered. "If something happens to you, I'll never forgive myself, your mother will never forgive me, the whole town of Jolly Mill—"

"Would you stop?" Lynley sat slumped low in the seat, and with the tinted windows in Gerard's SUV, they'd hoped to make this work. "We're doing the best we can, and you know I can handle that pistol in the glove compartment. Not that it'll come to that."

"No. I'll be with Dodge, and I'll have my eyes on him at all times. He'll never know you're anywhere in Cassville. I still think it might've been better for you to go with Gerard to Springfield than to be sitting in the car while I interrogate."

"Look at it this way—you need me to give you directions to the house."

"GPS."

"Your girlfriend?" Lynley's voice raised in mock exasperation, making him smile despite the reason for this trip.

"Just because it has a female voice—"

"And has gotten us lost half the time we've used her. Remember when she placed us on Highway 76 in Branson during rush hour? But would you listen to me and take the alternate routes? No, you had to listen to your girlfriend instead of your... good friend."

He grinned over at her and was glad to see it reflected back at him. Since reading that note yesterday and seeing her reaction to it, he'd felt overwhelmed with a need to cheer her up, to ensure her safety at any cost. She didn't realize that he could see the pain in her eyes when she thought her ex-husband might have threatened her life. To think that someone who had once vowed to love her might now be threatening to kill her...of course that would hurt.

"There's the first traffic signal," she said. "You'll want to turn left."

"You sure? Maybe I should ask my girlfriend."

She chuckled, and he felt warm all the way

through. Good. He'd gotten her to laugh. Mere hours after meeting her, he'd learned about her mistrust of every GPS system known to man. Lynley preferred a good old-fashioned map. She'd even challenged his GPS system to a test, and Lynley and her map had won. In Branson, Missouri, no less, which challenged every GPS system invented.

"Where's Kirstie?" he asked.

"Lunch prep at the rehab center. Nora and Carmen are guarding her, just in case. I hope Nora bakes some of her famous cookies while she's in the kitchen. I would've been helping if Gerard hadn't been called out."

"Now, that's something I'd like to see."

"What? Me cooking? I can do that."

"I've never seen it."

"That's because we're always at Mom's and she likes to cook."

"And you don't."

"Not my skill set."

"I recall a gluten-free puff pancake you made that was one of the best things I ever tasted. Oh, and that thing you call a man-quiche."

"That's right. I remember. You ate the whole thing."

"I have to admire a woman who knows her skill set."

She chuckled.

He felt a little squeeze in the region of his chest. It was a warning sign; Lynley had begun to settle even more deeply into his heart. It alarmed him now as it did every time he thought about it.

"Turn left again at the next road."

"How many times did we go over these directions before—"

"Now turn right. Trust me, it's a short, one-block street, and it's hard to—"

"Turn right here?"

"Left, then immediately right. Maybe you weren't listening."

"I could always have used the GPS."

"Someday she's going to disappear and you'll never find her."

"Oh, but I'll know who did the dastardly deed."

"That won't matter. You'll need proof."

"How many traffic signals did you say Cassville has?"

"Three, I believe."

He shook his head. "And you thought I'd get lost in a town this size?" He'd thought his hometown of Sikeston, Missouri, across the state, was small, but tiny farming communities were the norm in the Missouri Ozarks. The closest shopping mall was in Springfield, over an hour's drive from Jolly Mill.

The charm of a small town outclassed the convenience of the third-largest city in Missouri for

Lynley, however, and since she was a country girl at heart, she came home to stay with Kirstie whenever she didn't have back-to-back shifts at the hospital.

John smiled when he tried to count how many of Lynley's friends just happened to mention, with a wink, that she never used to come home so often. She'd been scheduled for two shifts this week, and neither John, Gerard nor Kirstie had been able to make her call the hospital and cancel those shifts yesterday.

Later last night, after Kirstie had gone to bed with an old rifle under her pillow and Gerard had gone home with his wife, John tried again.

"Lynley, I can't believe you," he'd said. "None of us can know when you might come under attack. It's foolhardy to attempt to work under these circumstances."

"Then come with me."

"You think the hospital will allow you to have a bodyguard all day?"

"No, because the hospital won't know about this threat."

"And why is that?" he asked.

"Because I won't tell them."

"That, too, is foolhardy. You need to consider your patients. They could be in danger, too."

Lynley picked up the note and shook it in his face. "You said this was written by someone who's greedy, not someone out for revenge. That means the hospital will be a safe place to be. So I'm going. End of argument."

"You know what? It's one thing to be strong and determined. It's dangerous to be as bullheaded and stubborn as a…an old bull." Great way with words, Russell.

And Lynley laughed. Which made John angry.

He got up and paced across the living room floor. "Sandra would never have done this."

He didn't realize he'd spoken the words aloud until he turned back to see Lynley's eyes widening and her lips parting. "Done what?" she asked softly. Too softly.

He sank into the recliner across the room from her. "Laughed at me for worrying about her safety."

"What would she have done?"

"She'd have done as I asked, even if she believed it was only for my own peace of mind."

In the long silence afterward, John realized he'd breached a deadly boundary. A man with any sense never compared the woman he was seeing with an ex-wife, a former girlfriend, his mother and especially not his late wife, whom he'd loved with all his heart.

"Then for your own peace of mind," Lynley said, her voice still soft, "you should remember I'm not your wife." She got up and went to bed.

Early this morning he found a note slipped beneath the guest room door where he had stayed with his Glock beneath the pillow. "Just so you know," the note said, "I'm *not* your wife, and you *don't* have a right to tell me what to do, but I *have* decided to take leave until after the first of the year."

He'd had to smother his laughter in his pillow. He'd folded the note and placed it into his billfold.

Lynley kept her mouth shut as John made two more turns. He'd been right—he didn't need her to sit beside him and direct. The man had an excellent sense of direction. He also had a comfortable way about him. They could sit together in silence and not be uncomfortable.

She, however, grew less comfortable the closer they got to her former home. Though she knew how to handle the weapon in the glove compartment, she'd never actually had to use one for self-protection. She couldn't go in with John, but she didn't want to sit in the car. And why was she so uncomfortable about that? It didn't make sense. John would be interviewing the only suspect they had, so it wasn't as if a prospective killer would be hanging around the car.

"Hey, I have an idea," she said. "You have your Bluetooth earpiece, right?"

He patted his pocket.

"And I have mine in my purse. Why don't we link up? If Dodge says something untrue, I can tell you. I can follow the interview that way."

He frowned. "Interesting thought. We might be in iffy territory, though. You're the victim, and a victim should never be in the same room as a suspect."

"I wouldn't be in the same room. He might think he's being recorded if he sees the earpiece, but he won't know I'm on the other end."

"Okay, get your earpiece out and call me when the time comes."

She let out a lungful of air she hadn't realized she was holding. "Thanks. I think I need that connection right now. I'm getting a little nervous."

"Just remember you've got me right here between the two of you. He can't get to you."

"I know." She always felt safe when she was with John. "Um...you remember that thing we argued about last night?"

"Which thing? We argued about more than one—"

"I'm talking about the main argument."

"Oh, you mean the one you wrote to me about this morning?"

She giggled, an embarrassing trait she had when stressed. "I heard you laughing. I think it woke Mom up."

"Sorry."

"No, I'm sorry, John. This is all so terrifying. I might behave like a cantankerous old bull, but I'm really scared."

He hesitated, glanced at her. "So am I."

"Not what I wanted to hear."

"Just being honest. We can't predict what's going to happen next. That's why we have to take everything so seriously and watch our every move."

"Yes. And I will. And you know that other… argument? You know, about my not being your… you know…your wife? I wasn't trying to be hateful at all."

"I knew that, Lynley."

"It's just that I learned at a young age not to let others control my life, and when I did, I was sorry."

"And the reason you're sorry is because of the person you married. Trust me, marriage to the right person? Totally different experience, I can assure you."

Despite the fact that she'd often encouraged him to talk about his wife and his marriage, this time his remark felt a little like a jab. As if maybe she'd made the wrong choice, and that was the only chance she'd ever have. Or that maybe Sandra really was the only woman for him. Ever. She pushed away the thought.

"If you hadn't been here yesterday," she said,

"I don't know what I'd have done. And about the marriage thing…"

"You don't have to explain that to me. I think we're both on the same page with that."

"Which would be…?"

"Which would be that I find you beautiful and exciting, Lynley." He glanced across at her, and his foot automatically eased from the accelerator.

She stared at him with parted lips.

"You're a definite temptation to abandon my lonely life, and I'm just now realizing how much of a temptation that is."

She caught her breath, ready to tell him the same thing. But she let him continue.

"Several weeks before Sandra died, she told me she wanted me to find a wonderful woman, someone who would make me happy. Her final wish was for me to remarry and raise a family."

"She was ri—"

"But I don't know if I'll ever be able to make her final wish come true."

Lynley couldn't believe the sting of disappointment she felt at his words.

"We'd been trying to do just that," he said. "Have a family. That was when we discovered her cancer."

Lynley swallowed. Hard. There was a thickness in her throat as she thought about the pain he'd endured. It was at that moment that she realized how very much John Russell had become entangled in her heart. When she would have expected to feel jealousy over his inability to recover from the death of his dead wife, she felt as if she was sharing his pain, instead. Although she felt rejected by his words, she also ached for his awful loss.

"I hate that," she said. Her voice caught, and she realized she was close to tears. For him. "I wish, for your sake, that Sandra had never gotten sick, that she'd lived and thrived and given you a whole house filled with happy children. I can't imagine a single unhappy child growing up in a household with parents like you and Sandra."

He stared straight ahead, hands turning white with his grip on the steering wheel. "Thank you, Lynley." It sounded as if he, too, was having some difficulty with thickness in his throat.

"I mean it. I know God knows what he's doing, but I'll never understand all the hardships we see. Not in this lifetime."

"While Sandra battled her cancer physically," John said, "I joined the same battle with prayer. I can't tell you how many times I fell asleep praying for her to heal, and then awakened with the same words on my lips."

"But God didn't answer your prayers."

"Not what I'd asked for at all, no."

Why, God?

Of course, she knew better than to ask. "God

allowed me to struggle many times in my life, and made me watch Mom's pain with my father's behavior. It seemed to happen to me more often than with most of my friends."

John looked at her. "But after your struggle to get past your anger, looking back you could see how you'd grown during those times."

"How'd you know?"

"The day Sandra died," John said, "I shut down."

She nodded.

"I was barely able to face the funeral—all those trite, unhelpful sayings I'd once blabbered, myself, for lack of knowing what else to say. You know the words…God had another plan for Sandra…God wanted her in heaven…she was better off now… it was God's will."

"I know the words well," she said softly.

"I cut myself off from friends and family. When the Russell clan started pressuring me too much to jump back into life and just 'get past it,' I turned off my phone and stopped answering when the doorbell rang."

"Did you get those who'd also lost loved ones that felt the need to load you down with their stories?"

"That, too."

"What did you do?" They'd never talked about this before. Until now, Lynley had kept the subject of Sandra's death off-limits, just as she'd kept the subject of her father's behavior off-limits.

"I asked for an interdepartmental transfer at work and changed churches. Even though I loved my church, they couldn't understand that I'd become a different person. I stopped teaching Sunday school, quit choir, stopped committee work, and they decided I'd lost my faith."

"And yet you didn't shut God out of your life."

"How could I shut out the One who is my reason for living? I feel as if I failed Sandra because I haven't followed up on her final request."

"Did she give you a time limit?"

He shook his head.

"Then don't worry so much," she said quietly. "I understand, John. Something in you died with Sandra, just as something in me died with the death of my marriage. Sometimes I feel there's too much pain from the past to risk the same in the future."

He shot her a glance. "Wow, we're perfect for each other, aren't we?"

She gave him a sad smile. "We both want solitude. I feel as if my comfort zone has been depleted. Even when I feel a strong desire to be a part of someone's life again—"

"You also feel a need to withdraw?" he said.

"Sometimes."

He flipped the turn signal. "Your friendship

has been a happy constant in my life since I first arrived in Jolly Mill. I could be mistaken, but it doesn't seem as if either of us has had a lot of that solitude lately."

She leaned back in her seat, surprised that she hadn't acknowledged that herself.

Was it time to put some distance between them, despite her growing attraction? She couldn't bear to be the cause of another devastation in his life. What if someone managed to get to her, even after all John's efforts?

"I didn't mention it in front of Mom yesterday," she said, searching for a change of subject, "but when Dodge and I moved here from Kansas City, it was so I could help take care of her. He once casually remarked that if Mom died we'd never have to work again."

John sucked in his breath.

"That broke the emotional ties I had with him. It was when I discovered he wasn't the person I believed him to be. I just didn't do anything about it until I had legal reason."

"Anything else he said that would lead you to believe he'd threaten your life for money?"

"Nothing he ever did or said implied he would threaten my life, John. Sure, he likes money. He doesn't like work. During the divorce proceedings he did ask for a piece of the inheritance he knew

Mom would receive, even though his own attorney rolled his eyes at that."

"You didn't mention that yesterday."

"I've tried so hard for so long to forget about his involvement in my life, these things slipped my mind. My father was the one who told Dodge about the money. Neither Mom nor I ever mentioned the extent of Uncle Lawson's personal finances because it was no one's business."

"Do you think Dodge remained in the area because he thought he might still get a grab at the money?"

"You mean by threatening my life? I might not be the best judge of human nature—obviously I'm not—but I can't bring myself to believe Dodge would spend this much of his life in the 'backwater' town, as he calls Cassville, just on the off chance that he might be able to swindle or threaten Mom into giving him money. Why not start robbing banks?"

"I need to know everything you know about Dodge, or about who else might have a reason to hurt you. This isn't gossip. It's self-preservation."

"All I can think of right now is that I walked in on him with another woman. I'd already heard from too many people about his affairs, and I was sick of it."

"So that's when you filed?"

"That's right."

"Will it disturb you to learn that I discovered this morning that he's snagged himself another woman—a neurologist who works in Joplin?"

"Why should it? He always did want to trade up financially. That leaves him even less likely to be the culprit. But it also means we might not catch him alone this morning."

"Not we. I. I might not catch him alone." John wrapped his Bluetooth earpiece around his ear. "You're not coming in with me."

"I know. You might not even catch him awake. It's early yet, and unless Dodge has changed, he sleeps late on his days off."

"I've already checked his schedule with the hospital, and he's off today." John glanced over at her. "Someday you'll have to tell me about your father."

Lynley stared out the window at the winter scenery, the patches of snow that were quickly melting. "He, too, had women." She paused. "He attempted to kill Mom with mercury in the air vent to make it look as if she developed premature Alzheimer's. And, like Dodge, he always attempted to seduce upwardly mobile women. Some desperate women with money could be generous to younger, attractive men."

"How did you know about all this?"

"Small town, lots of big mouths, though he tried hard to keep Mom from knowing. After all, he knew she would inherit, and he didn't want a divorce before that happened."

John slowed the SUV nearly to a stop in front of Lynley's former home. An older blue Ford was parked in front of a two-car garage. They sat and stared at it for a long, tense moment.

"There are a lot of blue cars on the road," she said.

"Did he have this when you divorced?"

"No. He had the pickup truck, silver. Maybe we should've brought Mrs. Drews so she could identify it."

"Take a picture with your cell, then link us up." He made a U-turn and parked beneath the bare overhanging branches of a maple tree. He situated them just right so Lynley couldn't be seen from the house. "Just sit and listen."

Lynley sighed. "Having one's life threatened can be so confining."

"You'll adapt." He paused, adjusting the sound on his earpiece. "You know, tastes can mature over time."

She screwed up her face as she tried to follow his subject change, but he'd lost her. "What?"

"You think you'd still be attracted to a man like Dodge?"

"Absolutely not, no way, never in a million years."

He chuckled. "See what I mean? Tastes change."

"I didn't take the time to get to know Dodge. I think I found myself drawn to him because he was the opposite of my father—or so I thought. Not physically appealing to other women. Little did I know what some women would go for."

"I'm sorry you had to find out about him the way you did."

"The problem was that I never had any deep conversations with him," Lynley said. "He was an extrovert, liked to be around a lot of people all the time. I thought that would be good for me, but it meant we weren't alone much when we were dating. You and I have had more deep conversations in one month than he and I had throughout our whole marriage. He was smart enough, he just wasn't a deep thinker."

"I'm a deep thinker?"

"Most certainly. We talk about more than the weather, and you don't try to make small talk because you're uncomfortable with the silence, or afraid I'm mad at you for some reason if I'm quiet for more than five minutes."

"Sounds as if Dodge had a guilty conscience."

"Too bad I figured that out after the wedding."

John studied the house. "Hey, did you say you painted the trim?"

She turned, at last, to view the house she'd tried so hard to make a home. And had failed. The antique brick, deep green Victorian trim that matched the fence, the landscaping she'd worked so hard to grow. It didn't appear Dodge had done anything to keep it up. Old, brown vines covered half the house number, and leaves beneath the trees were at least four inches deep. "I built the backyard privacy fence myself."

He whistled. "You do good work. Too bad nobody bothered with upkeep."

"Yeah, too bad."

"I'll let you help me build my fence as soon as I buy the supplies. You did this all by yourself?"

"Mom taught me how. It never was my father's thing."

"Perfect," he said. "You ready?"

"I'm scared. Be careful."

"You think your ex can beat me up?"

"No, but—"

"I'll be careful. If he's guilty I'll see him behind bars no matter the cost."

Lynley closed her eyes, praying John's words were true, while at the same time praying that Dodge wasn't the culprit at all. Not because she continued to carry any residual love for him, but because she'd already grown up with one man who'd attempted to kill her mother. What kind of damage would it do to her soul if she'd been married to a man who now wanted her dead?

FIVE

John took a few snapshots of the car in the drive-way, then called in the license plate number. Sure enough, word came back momentarily that the blue car belonged to Dodge Knowles. Apparently he no longer owned the truck Lynley mentioned.

Sliding his cell phone into his back pocket, John hesitated on the front porch of the antiqued brick house. The place appeared to have at least three bedrooms, maybe four. Lynley must have purchased it with the intention of filling it with children.

A curtain moved in the front picture window, then the curtain slid open. John studied it. No more movement followed.

He pressed the doorbell button, didn't hear a chime, decided that was another thing the man hadn't kept in working order. He knocked.

The door opened almost immediately and a slender man with light brown, slept-in hair stood blinking at him. Lynley had said that Dodge didn't typically rise before noon unless he was working.

The man squinted in the sunlight. "Thought I heard a car out here."

John winced at the guy's morning breath. "I'm Police Chief John Russell from Jolly Mill, Missouri." He showed his credentials and saw the man's eyes widen in surprise. "Are you Dodge Knowles?"

The guy's light brown eyes appeared empty of guile, but he would have to be a talented actor to fool Lynley long enough to get her to marry him. "That's me."

John read nothing but curiosity in the man's expression. He had a boyish face and a certain look of cluelessness. "May I come in for a moment? I'd like to ask you some questions."

Dodge scratched his head and yawned as he stepped back and drew the door open. He wore nothing but a pair of baggy cutoff denim shorts.

John swallowed and breathed, wishing he could stand farther away from morning-breath man. He followed Dodge inside and looked around the nicely furnished great room.

"Dodge, who's there?" came a woman's voice down a wide hallway that must have led to the bedrooms.

"Just a guy who wants to talk to me. You can stay in bed."

John wondered briefly at Dodge's failure to tell her there was a cop in the house, and then he wondered if Lynley had heard the exchange.

A door shut softly. Dodge gestured to a plush sofa and sank into a leather recliner. He grabbed a throw pillow from the sofa and hugged it to himself—possibly feeling exposed without a shirt? Or was he subconsciously worried about a different kind of exposure?

John hesitated and sat. Either this guy was a consummate actor, or he didn't have any idea why he was getting this visit.

"Mr. Knowles, have you been in contact with your ex-wife, Lynley Marshall, in the past few days?"

To John's surprise, the man's face creased with the first signs of worry. "Lynley? You're here about her? No. Why? Is she okay?" He leaned forward. "Nothing's happened to her, has it?"

John paused for a moment to study and wait for Lynley to make any remarks. She remained silent, and the only way he knew she was still connected was the sound of her breathing. He'd learned years ago that it was sometimes easier to get information from someone if you just shut up and let them talk a little.

"Chief?" Dodge leaned forward. "She's not hurt or anything, is she? Has there been an accident?"

"No accidents." The poor guy was going to have

to stew, because there was no way John would tell him about the note. "You haven't spoken to her on the phone or had any other kind of communication with her in the past few months?"

Dodge shook his head, looking almost like a clueless, unkempt pup. Almost. "I tried to call her a couple of times." He spoke softly enough not to be heard outside the great room. Fortunately, he leaned closer to John. Lynley would be able to hear him.

"Mom told me he called," came her soft voice over the earpiece. "She wouldn't give him my new cell phone number."

John nodded. "Any reason for trying to contact her?"

"You know…a fella has regrets. I thought maybe we could at least be friends. She never would return my calls. Or maybe her mother never gave her the messages. She didn't like me. But I guess I wasn't always a likeable person."

Lynley inhaled sharply, but she said nothing.

Once again, John found himself speechless with amazement. Lynley Marshall, sharp and ambitious, had actually married this man? John found it hard to believe.

But John didn't always understand the dynamics of relationships. He'd had to study books on the subject in order to better grasp how to deal with perpetrators and suspects on the job, and their family dynamics. A criminal psychologist he was not.

Unfortunately, although this suspect hadn't appeared suspicious at first glance, things could always change. Maybe it had been a good idea to allow Lynley to play fly-on-the-wall with the Bluetooth connection. "Have you been approached by someone who wanted to discuss Lynley in the last few weeks?"

Dodge hesitated for a split second too long.

"I take it you have?" John pressed. "Perhaps Lynley or her mother became the subject of one or more of your recent conversations with friends or acquaintances over the Christmas holidays? Maybe at the hospital where you work? After all, didn't you and Lynley work together at your present place of employment?"

Dodge leaned forward. "Say, you been keeping tabs on me? What's going on?"

"I'm sorry, but this is my investigation, not yours. Has someone contacted you about your past marriage to Lynley?"

"Our marriage? Uh, no. That ended more than two years ago." Dodge shook his head, appearing confused. "Why would they do that? I mean, I haven't carried on a decent conversation with her since the day our divorce became final, and I wouldn't exactly call that a decent conversation. Her bulldog attorney wouldn't let me near her."

"Again, not what I asked."

"You know, I wasn't the one who filed for divorce. What's she doing, coming back after the house?"

"The terms of your divorce are not in question here."

"Oh. Well, good. 'Cause she'll be swimming in money soon enough."

Lynley made a few sounds of frustration over the earpiece.

"Do you have some reason to believe that?" John asked.

The man's face scrunched. "Sure. Everybody knows she had the rich great-uncle that was ready to kick off at any time."

"He's still a greedy dog," Lynley said softly.

John had to prevent himself from nodding his head automatically. "And how much money would that entail?" John pulled out his pad and pen and jotted a few notes.

"Her dad told me her mom's old uncle was worth millions. The guy didn't have any kids of his own, so it was all going to Kirstie and her brother. When he died, that was it for our marriage, you could just tell. Lynley didn't want to share."

"Let me come in there," Lynley muttered. "Let him say that to my face."

"No." John knew his answer to Lynley might

confuse Dodge. He quickly recovered. "I've heard too many husbands cry foul after a divorce. The least you can do is be a man about it and tell me the truth."

Dodge held his gaze for a moment, then looked toward the hallway, where someone in the bedroom might also be listening. "Okay, I can't place all the blame on her for our dead marriage. I knew we weren't meant for each other before the wedding ever took place. I like women. It's not something I'm proud of, and I'm not proud of the fact that they like me." He shrugged. "Don't ask me why."

"But you married her anyway, knowing you wouldn't be faithful?"

"Well, I got to know her dad, and he let slip about Kirstie's uncle."

"So you're saying you married her for a future inheritance?"

Dodge grimaced, cleared his throat, and had the grace to blush. "It isn't as if I didn't like her. And she liked me quite a bit. Of course, it kinda made things iffy when her ol' pop warned me not to even try to get my hands on the money, because he had plans for it."

John looked at his notes. "My records tell me Barry Marshall is no longer living."

"Yeah, and you know why? I think he got too greedy. It's one thing to let the ladies pitch in every so often, but it's not cool to try to cut them out of their inheritance. Guy turned out to be a jerk."

"So you believe he got what he deserved?"

"Sure do."

"What about you? Think you'd ever do something illegal to get your hands on money you wanted for yourself?"

Dodge jerked backward, almost overacting. "What? You can't mean that. What kind of a guy do you think I am?"

"I think you're the kind of man who would ask for a piece of your mother-in-law's inheritance in divorce court."

"You've been talking to Lynley?"

"That's irrelevant."

"But what are you doing here?" Dodge frowned, the wrinkles around his eyes revealing his age more than anything John had seen yet. "Is somebody contesting the will? Or what about that big ol' lawsuit? You think they're going after Lynley since the court didn't give in?"

John felt as if he held a fishing rod out over the bank of a river, and a big fish had just nibbled at the bait. "What do you think?"

Dodge blinked, but didn't hold John's gaze. He darted a surreptitious glance down the hallway, where his woman waited for John to leave. Or she'd gone back to sleep. Or she was listening, and Dodge didn't want her to hear. He scooted closer to

John and gestured for him to lean closer—something John did with extreme reluctance. Perhaps he could offer the man a mint.

"Okay, I'll admit it, I blew it with Lynley, okay? But I wouldn't hurt her, not for all the money in the world."

"Would you threaten to?"

The man's widening eyes could almost convince John he was sincere. "No! You're talking about physically hurting her? What on earth is going on here? Is someone threatening to hurt Lynley?"

"Mr. Knowles, have you been keeping up with the lawsuit?" And why was he so interested in whether his woman friend heard them talking? What would his housemate know? Maybe she would be a good lead to follow up on later.

Dodge sniffed, looked at John, raised an eyebrow. "Speaking of Lynley, am I going nuts, or do I smell her perfume?" He leaned closer to John. "Have you been…with her?" And then he glanced out the window at the SUV, got up and walked to look out, his skinny legs seeming like toothpicks sticking out from his overly baggy shorts. "Is she out there?" he called over his shoulder.

"Oh, no, John," Lynley said into his ear. "Don't let him see me."

"Mr. Knowles." John gave his voice a hard edge. "I'm not finished interviewing you. Please be seated."

For a moment, Dodge hesitated, still watching the SUV with his eyes narrowed. "She is. I know that smell of lilacs and powder. She always wore it when she wasn't working. She loved that stuff."

John nodded. "And she's the only woman in the world, of course, who would wear this specific scent?"

Dodge wandered back to the chair he'd abandoned. "Well, it's for sure you wouldn't be wearing it, and it's a scent for an old lady, so yes. Lynley's the only one I know."

In the earpiece, Lynley sighed. "I forgot he has a tendency to pick up on certain things. Sorry. I guess I sprayed a little liberally this morning."

"Look, are you going to tell me what's going on here?" Dodge asked.

"Sorry. I'm not at liberty to share the details of an ongoing investigation at this time," John said, keeping his voice as professional and friendly as he knew how. He was thankful for the experience he'd had with police investigations, though he had to admit to himself that he'd changed his style a little since moving to Jolly Mill, which was much more laid-back. "Has anyone emailed you for information about Lynley, or used any other form of communication to ask you about her? Or has she contacted you, herself?"

"What?" came Lynley's voice.

John ignored it.

Dodge lowered his head and leaned in again, a sure sign he was about to speak softly once more. "Only one who's asked me about her was Tara." He glanced down the hallway, then jerked his head toward the closed door. "That's just jealousy talking, 'cause Lynley's younger and...uh..." He glanced again toward the door. "Prettier," he whispered. "Not that Tara's a dog or anything, but...well, you've seen Lynley, right? When are you going to tell me whether or not she's safe?"

John relented. "She's safe."

"Well, make sure you keep it that way." Dodge hesitated and switched his attention to the hallway again.

"You can help with that."

"I want to, but how? I still care about her, you know. We could've been great together if she'd only given me another chance."

Sure they could have. John pressed his teeth together to keep from saying that out loud.

When Dodge had first opened the front door, his shaggy, light brown hair and ingenuous expression had made him seem younger than he obviously was. Now the light coming in through decorative, pastel stained-glass window panels on each side of the door showed more obvious lines around his eyes, and his unkempt hair had some strands of white at the temples. If he was living with an older woman, how much older was she?

"Lynley was pretty young when you met her?" John asked.

Dodge gave a quick frown, as if he couldn't quite figure out why the slight change in subject. "Eight years younger than me. I was a nurse, just like her, except I was an LPN and she was an RN, but although she made more money, I was happy with my job."

"And she wanted more, of course," John said, suddenly filling his voice with compassion, male bonding and all that. "Did she keep at you to take extra courses so you could bring in more money?"

"You're dead meat, John Russell." Lynley's voice was only slightly teasing.

The scruffy man frowned at him. "No. She's not like that. She just wanted help with housework and stuff while she took night courses."

"See?" Lynley said. "Told you."

John was suddenly sorry he'd agreed to her harebrained idea. He'd know better next time.

"Where did you two meet? I'd like to cover as much as possible. You'd be surprised how many clues might rise to the surface." Now that he was tempted to dismiss the raggedy man as a suspect, he might get something helpful from him.

"Saint Luke's in Kansas City."

"You both worked there together?"

Dodge stretched his neck and shifted in his seat. Good. He was getting fussy. "Yeah, until Kirstie got cancer and Lynley insisted on moving closer to home to help take care of her."

"How did that make you feel?" John asked.

Dodge shrugged. "I didn't think it'd take so long, and there are always job ops for nurses, you know. But then Lynley wanted to buy this place, and she used some money she'd set aside. She spent a lot of time with her mother, and I figured, hey, sure, that was a good idea, since Kirstie's always shown her appreciation for stuff like that. You know. Financially. If we needed money, Kirstie came through, though Lynley hardly ever let her. I really did blow it, you know?"

"Especially since she was going to inherit millions?"

Dodge shrugged. "Not just that."

"Do you recall where you first heard about Barry Marshall's demise?" John needed a name. Just another name to track.

Dodge glanced again toward the hallway. "Actually, I just found out recently. Shocked me. I mean, I keep up, you know, with news and stuff. Nobody from the family ever bothered to tell me Barry was dead. I found out from Tara."

John could practically feel Lynley's sucked-in breath over the Bluetooth. He felt his own stomach twist in that way it did when he was onto a lead and couldn't exactly say why. Except this time it was pretty obvious. "So Tara was a friend of the family that long ago?" He kept his voice casual.

Dodge snorted and shook his head. "A friend of Barry's only. A good friend." He leaned close and winked.

"Did you and Tara know each other before Barry's death, then?"

"Sure did. I met her the same time Barry did, at the hospital in Joplin when Kirstie was getting set up for chemo treatments."

John wished Lynley hadn't heard that. Barry Marshall made time with a woman while his wife battled cancer? With a flash of guilt, John felt glad the man was dead. No, one couldn't call Barry Marshall a man. He was a piece of trash.

"Uh, you okay?" Dodge asked.

Sometimes John regressed. Time to get back to the present.

"Is Tara your wife?" John asked.

Dodge grimaced and shook his head, as if John had said something distasteful. "She, uh, well, we met up again a few months ago. That was when she told me Barry was dead." He shook his head. "I've always had a thing for women docs."

"Where'd you meet up?"

"Singles bar up in Joplin. I knew a lot of the docs went there, what with plenty of medical folk up that way. I bought her a drink, we got to talking, and…well…turns out her lease on an apartment was up soon, and she was looking for a temporary place to stay before her house was finished. You know the tornado that took a third of Joplin out a few years ago? She lost her home to that. I felt sorry for her, and so..." He spread his hands. "Next thing I knew, she'd moved in. You're not going to tell me why you're asking all these questions, are you?"

"Sorry. I would if I could, but—"

"Okay, okay, got it. But I didn't do anything, okay?"

"You know how it is. Ever seen the police procedurals on TV? We've got to go back over and over—"

He heard a gasp over his earpiece, and then Lynley cried out. "John? Help!"

SIX

A buzz set in Lynley's ears as she stared down the barrel of a huge revolver—it appeared to be a .357. She switched her attention to the face of the woman who leaned forward, holding her gaze with eyelashes that looked like glued-on tarantula legs. That was the first point of recognition. The hospital. This was the doctor. Other familiarities hit Lynley like pellets to her heart. This was Tara, the woman living with Dodge. She'd been one of Dad's...women.

Clenching and unclenching her fists, Lynley fought back her fury and allowed common sense to take control. Fear was a wise emotion to have right now. Why couldn't she experience that?

Because her anger outweighed it all.

Lynley was so focused on that weapon, and the makeup-coated snake holding it, that she didn't know until Tara shot a nervous glance toward the street that John was running toward them, his own weapon drawn. Their voices might have been raised enough for Lynley to hear them, but because of the buzzing in her ears—okay, that had to be from the fear she didn't think she was feeling—she couldn't make out their words.

She watched John slow his pace as he neared the SUV, and then Dodge burst out of the house behind him, eyes wide with horror, yelling at the top of his lungs, angrily.

"Tara, what are you doing? Where did you find my gun? Drop that thing. Now!" His voice could have easily reached across all of Cassville.

Tara kept her weapon trained on Lynley and shouted back, "You want her to die, come closer."

Lynley glanced at the glove compartment, but the woman wouldn't look away long enough for her to do anything. John continued to move toward the SUV until he was at the front door. Lynley hadn't locked herself in. She'd intended to. But that wouldn't have mattered with a .357 aimed at her head from less than a foot away. The window wasn't unbreakable, and no one would miss a shot at her head from this distance.

The weapon moved briefly, but only when the back door opened. Lynley saw from the rearview mirror when Tara slunk into the vehicle, the lethal revolver still held inches from Lynley's head. The buzzing had stopped. She felt the fear clearly now, all through her body in tremors that made her weak. She couldn't move away from the woman even if she had the chance.

Dodge stood in the middle of the street, frozen, eyes bugged out with horror, hands at his sides. "You're crazy, Tara. You think you can get away with this?"

Tara laughed. "Thanks for all your help, little man. You've made everything so much easier." With the help of the information Dodge gave John, Lynley remembered that voice, and recalled seeing her father standing at the end of the corridor where Mom was staying after her surgery. Their silhouettes mocked her, even now when she closed her eyes. Their heads had been close together. Intimate.

"Chief," Tara called out of the open door. "Get into the car and drive, and if you don't throw that gun across the road into the perfect yard that Dodge's precious ex-wife planted with such care, I'll blow her brains all over this nice, clean interior."

John tossed the weapon and slowly opened the door. His light green eyes were steady and filled with reassurance as he held Lynley's gaze. "You okay?"

She shook her head.

A shadow streaked past the back window. Lynley heard footsteps, heard Dodge's voice, and then suddenly an explosion blasted through the rear window of the vehicle, glass shattering around them. Dodge screamed and fell backward into the leaves to the right of the SUV. Lynley reached for the door.

John grabbed her arm and held her.

She tried to jerk away. "What are you doing? She shot him!"

"I'll shoot you next, little lady," came the hard female voice behind her as she brushed pieces of glass from her clothes. "A limb at a time. Now, Chief, drive as if your life depended on it, because it does."

"I'm not leaving a man to bleed to death," John said.

"So you want your darling Lynley to bleed instead?" She pulled back the hammer. "Hair trigger, here. I know, because Dodge taught me how to shoot it. Don't worry, I won't kill her. I'll wound her so badly she'll wish she'd never lived, but I have too much at stake to kill her. You, though. You I can kill."

John looked sick when he fastened his seat belt, punched the accelerator and lurched the SUV forward, looking in his rearview mirror with shadowed eyes.

"Is he moving?" Lynley's voice shook so badly it came out in a whisper.

"I can't tell." He glared into the rearview mirror at Tara. "You call yourself a doctor?"

"I am a doctor. I have an IQ at least twice as high as yours, and I've helped more pathetic, needy people than I care to remember. I'm sick of it. I've earned a break, but you know what? A tornado changed all that, took my mansion, took my office. A greedy patient sued me, and then another, until my insurance company dumped me. You won your case while I lost everything. I'm tired of helping the poor, pathetic losers of this world only to be turned on when they refuse to follow my orders. It's time I help myself for once."

Lynley watched John squeeze the steering wheel. Tara was telling on herself. Not that there was anything they could do with this information except get a better understanding of her mind-set.

"And where are we going?" he asked.

"Why, to Jolly Mill, of course. We're playing my game now, and soon we'll be depositing four million dollars into my offshore account. My money. That I earned."

"Helping Barry Marshall to poison his wife," John said.

"I'm an expert, after all. And he asked for my expertise."

"To murder my mother," Lynley said, praying silently that Dodge wasn't dead. "You're a vile, evil woman. You're no doctor, you're a killer. And there is no money."

A long silence from the backseat made Lynley's heart begin to beat faster. "You're a liar."

"My mother never inherited a cent. It all went to charity at her request."

The seat jerked with a kick from the back. "Not what I heard."

"You listened to the wrong people."

"Both Barry and Dodge told me about the money."

"Such trustworthy informants," Lynley said.

"Dodge only knew what Barry told him," John said. "When Barry died, he knew nothing about Kirstie's request that all her inheritance go to a homeless charity."

"That's crazy!" Tara shrieked. "Nobody turns down millions of dollars just to give it to worthless street people. Nobody's that stupid!"

Lynley's whole body tensed. Something in the woman's voice sounded…off. John looked over at Lynley and gave the barest shake of his head.

"You're going to call your mommy and tell her to transfer the money to my account. You're going to tell her where you are, and where I am, and what I'm holding to the back of your head." Tara's voice wobbled. "And you're going to warn her that if she tries to lie her way out of this, her little girl's going to lose her big, strong protector."

"How can she get money to you that she doesn't have?" Lynley felt a bit of her old anger kick back in and take over. "Do you know why my mother asked for the money to go elsewhere in the first place? Because she suspected her husband, my father, was poisoning her, and she was determined he wouldn't prosper from it."

"Call her. Now."

Lynley pretended to tap the Bluetooth on her ear and spoke her mother's name clearly while pulling her cell phone from her purse out of Tara's sight. If she'd been alone, she'd have reached for the glove compartment and the .22 Mag and taken her chances against Tara's superior firepower, but not with John within such close range. His ears, and his heart, probably also still rang with the shot that had downed Dodge.

"Okay, it's ringing, but she probably won't answer," Lynley said, hoping her voice would cover the sound of her text to Megan.

"She'd be working in the kitchen, probably serving and eating with the others right now, and she won't bother to answer her phone." She texted, "Trouble! Have Gerard call John."

She slid the phone over so John could see the text.

"What are you doing up there?" Tara demanded.

"Waiting!" Lynley snapped back. "I told you she probably wouldn't answer."

"She'd better. Your life depends on it."

* * *

John glanced at Tara Harkins, studying her, trying to get some kind of idea what could possibly be going through her mind. She was overly made-up, with red hair, a tiger-striped jumpsuit that left little to the imagination, and when she met his gaze she gave him a wink. She made his skin crawl.

"Don't try anything with me, doll." Her gaze roamed over his face. "You can't get out of this without risking your lovely lady's life." Her eyes filled with disgust as she glanced at the back of Lynley's seat. "Even I can see she's more to you than a simple victim of…circumstance."

Lynley cast him a quick glance.

"You're driving eighty, moron!" Tara yelled. "Trying to get us pulled over? I'm the one with the weapon."

"It doesn't bother you that you left the man who cared about you bleeding on the side of the street?" John asked.

"Should it? As soon as he found out his ex-wife might be in some kind of trouble, it was Ol' Scruffy to the rescue," she drawled. "As if. Poor little man's never gotten over her."

"I hadn't noticed," John said.

"He still keeps a picture of the two of them in his cell phone." She watched John's face closely. "Looks like I might've hit a nerve, Chief Russell.

What is it about this Lynley Marshall that keeps men so entranced?"

John caught the hostility in the woman's voice when she said Lynley's name. He had to be careful with this one. She likely hated Lynley for her youth and beauty.

"You don't know anything about me," Lynley said.

"The question is what don't I know about you?" she asked with a sweep of her gun. "I know you redecorated that whole house with your own able hands, and the front and back lawns are filled with lush foliage Dodge's dear little Lynley planted with a green thumb, which you've apparently always had. I know you kept men on a tight leash, from your daddy to your hubby, and now, it appears, to the chief, here." Tara pouted up at John. "Isn't that right?"

"Tight leash," John said. "As in, she expected fidelity from the men she knew? Is there something irrational about that?"

They were halfway to Jolly Mill when John's cell phone rang. He tapped his Bluetooth and answered without waiting for identification. "Kirstie? Your timing is impeccable."

"You on speaker?" It was Gerard's voice.

John didn't look in the rearview mirror, where he could so easily see the woman behind Lynley. "No, why?" It was nearly impossible to keep his voice calm, but apparently so far he was managing to fool spider-eyes.

"Dodge called the police. We know."

John felt a flood of relief. Dodge was alive.

"Speakerphone!" Tara shouted. "Now. Not another word until I can hear the conversation."

"Brace yourselves. Roadblock ahead. Switching to Megan," Gerard said quickly, just before John hit Speaker so their voices would be heard throughout the car.

"So you think the money can be wired?" John asked.

"I'll see to it," came Megan's voice.

"You'd better," Tara called to the speaker.

The phone disconnected.

Tara kicked the back of Lynley's seat again. Hard. "And you said there wasn't any money."

"As we said, all the money that would have gone to Kirstie went to charity instead." John had to keep her talking, distracted, while at the same time, he had to make sure he and Lynley would be safe. It was obvious now that the woman had lost her mind. "So what you're doing is stealing money from people who desperately need it."

"And yet, suddenly it's appeared," she crooned. "It's like...oh, I don't know, fate?"

"No," Lynley said. "It's more like greed, avarice, ignorance."

John could see her bracing for another kick

against the seat, but it didn't come. Instead, when John looked in the rearview mirror, he saw those hideous eyes narrow, and then a slow smile grew across the woman's face, appearing to crack the thick makeup in some places.

"I think it's more like death. This is a kidnapping, and I chose the right person to kidnap, didn't I? Everybody loves Lynley," she said in a high, singsong voice. "Everybody does whatever it takes to save Lynley, even if it means stealing from a charity to pay off her debt."

"I don't owe a debt." Lynley's right hand inched toward the glove compartment, and John felt his gut clench. No!

"You're the one who owes the debt," he said with a glance in the rearview mirror. "You're the neurologist, so you worked with Lynley's father, didn't you? You told him exactly what to do to make her mother develop Alzheimer's symptoms. You're the one with the debt. You owe her mother years of life."

"And yet, guess who's paying?"

"The homeless," he said. "But you, who have been earning good money with your profession, suddenly decided you deserved a stranger's money?"

"I didn't decide it. Barry did. He told me it would be ours as soon as Kirstie was gone. Her cancer was a bad one...well, bad for her. It could've been good for us if she hadn't fought so hard."

Lynley gasped. "That's why he stayed." She stopped reaching for the glove compartment and hugged her chest. "Of course. All this time I thought he stayed because he cared something for her. He'd never shown love before, so why when she was sick and an inconvenience for him?"

Lynley started again to reach for the glove compartment, but John placed a hand on her shoulder and squeezed.

She looked up at him.

He smiled despite their predicament. "She's right about one thing, you know."

"What's that?"

"There's something about you, Lynley Marshall. I'm thinking maybe Sandra would have approved of you."

"Who's this?" Tara snapped. "Are you two talking in code?"

"Not at all," John said. "Sandra was my late wife. She always wanted me to remarry and have a family. She lost the same battle Kirstie won. Until Lynley showed up in my life, I wasn't sure I'd be able to grant Sandra's dying wish."

"If you don't shut up, I'll make you." Tara glared at him in the rearview mirror. He held her gaze until he saw a road grader speeding toward the highway from a side road. It was coming fast. Too fast. This was Gerard's plan? He let up on the accelerator and automatically checked to make sure Lynley's seat belt was fastened. As always, it was. He'd noted earlier that Tara's was not. She needed room to move around in case they tried to break away from her.

The grader shot out into the road ahead of them. He hesitated just long enough to make a difference, and he prayed for safety and perfect timing, terrified for his and Lynley's lives.

Calling on his defensive driving classes last year, he slammed the brake as hard as he could. When the tires squealed and the SUV nosed to the right, he turned the wheel in the same direction to keep from skidding.

When he righted it and straightened, he tried to enter the oncoming lane, but there was an eighteen-wheeler in the way.

Instead, he aimed toward the ditch, bounced through it to the other side, his right arm automatically flying out to protect Lynley.

Bare branches of trees slapped the windshield until a barbed wire fence stopped them with an abruptness that launched white pops of air and powder.

SEVEN

The echo of screeching brakes, the hideous punch of the air bag and then sudden silence shocked Lynley into a physical freeze. She couldn't move, couldn't cry out, couldn't open her eyes. She felt a hand on her shoulder, felt the cool breeze of fresh air kiss her face, heard voices as if from far away. For a moment, she couldn't speak, couldn't think about how to react.

"Lynley?" John's arm—was that John's arm?— came around her and her seat belt released. She felt others approaching from her open door—someone had opened the door?

Other sounds came at her, the sound of an engine from heavy machinery. Yes, the road grader. She opened her eyes and could barely see past white powder. The air bag. Her shoulder hurt. Seat belt burn?

She saw John's hands as he brushed the powder from her face and shoulders, and then she saw red. Real red. Blood red.

Her mouth opened but nothing came out. She looked at John to make sure he wasn't the one bleeding. He was white, not red. She reached up to wipe at the powder on him.

He caught her hand and held it, and held her gaze. "Lynley. Tell me what hurts."

All she could do was shake her head. Nothing bad. "The...blood? Where..."

"She hit the seat hard back here," someone said from outside and behind.

"Hear those sirens?" someone else asked. "How'd they know?"

"Gerard Vance would have called," John said, his gaze still on Lynley. "Did you feel any sharp pain in your neck or back?"

She shook her head. "No pain. I felt as if I fell into a pillow top mattress at a hundred miles an hour."

"I think we need to call a coroner," came a voice from behind them.

Lynley knew, then. The blood. It was Tara's. It appalled her that she felt no horror, but neither did she feel relief that the woman threatening to do her worst to them had been stopped in such a horrendous way. She felt only sadness that a life was permanently destroyed.

"She's gone," John told her softly, his hand grasping hers. "You're safe."

She looked at him. "And so are you. I thought..."

John, I thought she was going to kill you and take me with her and—"

"I believe you're right. But it's over. Now, don't try to move. Just in case, I want you to get checked out in the ER."

"No need. I'm a nurse, remember? Been doing a ton of triage lately. You slowed us down enough, and the fence gave enough, I don't think we could have been seriously injured. Not belted in like this." She refused to look behind her. "And as it happens, I do want out of here as soon as the ambulance crew gets here and checks us out. I just want to go home."

John tapped his earpiece, spoke Gerard's name, waited. In seconds, Gerard picked up. "Hey, nice plan, pal. You'll be relieved to know that we had a safe landing." He waited a moment while Gerard spoke, then said, "Yes, I did tell you about that driving course. Just a couple of days ago, if I remember correctly. You have a lot of faith in my abilities. Kirstie's on her way with you? Good. I think Lynley just wants to go home. No, no hospital visit. We're both fine. Our abductor, however, didn't fare so well. Have you heard how Dodge is doing?" He waited, nodded, gave Lynley the thumbs-up. "He'll be fine."

She stared at John, wondering why she didn't even feel a sense of relief. She suddenly didn't care about anything.

John frowned at her and disconnected quickly. "Hey, you sure you're okay?" He took her hand again.

She squeezed it, and felt her whole body sucking up its warmth. She didn't want to let go, and he must have read her mind because he didn't. He held on.

"I think I'm still seeing a few final pieces of my life flash before my eyes." It surprised her that her voice was once again shaky, barely there.

"You've been delving far too deeply into your past," John said. There was a quaver to his voice, as well.

"No one should ever have to do that. Not like this. I'm so sorry you had to see all those ugly things about me...my life."

He looked down at their clasped hands. "You don't see it, do you?"

She frowned up at him, feeling increased warmth from him.

"Your strength," he said. "Your beauty. Your goodness."

For a moment she couldn't catch her breath, but she smiled at him, wishing she never had to let him go. She was tempted to warn him that he was seeing things that weren't there, but that would sound as if she was begging for more compliments.

"I see your mother's integrity in you, Lynley

Marshall. I also see your own independent spirit, your faith in God, your lovely…very lovely heart."

Her lips parted, and she struggled to say it. She must remind him. "My father's blood also runs through—"

"Whatever was wrong with your father must have happened in his mind alone, because it isn't in you."

"You can't know that."

"Let me be the judge of what I do and do not see in you." He took her hand in both of his and held tightly, then kissed it. "Your father's redeeming quality was you. I'll forever be glad he existed because you were born."

She blinked sudden tears from her eyes and looked down at their hands, and she felt so much tenderness for this man. So this was love. It was truly a function of God's grace.

Lynley's cell phone rang and she used her free hand to answer, unwilling to release John.

"How are you?"

"Oh, Mom." Lynley had never felt so relieved to hear her mother's voice.

Mom burst into tears.

"I'm okay. Better than okay." Lynley looked at John when she said it. "Didn't Gerard tell you? John and I are safe. I'm glad John drove Gerard's SUV today because it's built like a spaceship."

"I'm with Gerard and Megan." Mom sniffed. "I was so terrified."

"I know. Me, too."

"We'll be there as quickly as we can. Actually, the way Gerard's driving, maybe quicker."

Lynley hesitated. "We'll talk about it all when you get here, but our abductor is dead."

Mom said nothing.

"Did you hear me?"

"Yes. I just wanted to hear your voice."

"I know."

"I…I'll see you soon."

Even after years of witnessing the aftermaths of dozens of deadly automobile accidents, John still had trouble looking at them. Since this wasn't his jurisdiction, he allowed the first responders and Department of Transportation—which had loaned the police the road grader—to take the lead on this one.

He sat holding Lynley's hand, wishing he could hold her in his arms, instead. A crew gently and quietly removed Tara's body from the backseat.

After the ambulance crew helped John and Lynley from the SUV, they led them over to the ambulance and sat them down, questioned them, tested reflexes, looked them over as much as possible, and when John and Lynley both declined a trip to the hospital, the crew understood.

John reached into the back of the SUV and pulled out a blanket, led Lynley several yards from the activity and wrapped the blanket around both of them while they waited for Gerard.

"The police will want to question us," she said.

"I'll give them a full report," he said. "I'm not leaving you right now."

She looked up at him and smiled. "Sandra would be proud."

"Sandra would be spitting mad at what happened to you."

"Well, I am too. In fact, at first I didn't realize I was afraid. Sometimes my anger takes over at inconvenient moments."

He glanced over at the crowd that had gathered to help with the cleanup. A considerable number of rubberneckers slowed down to see the sight, and some of the DOT personnel took it upon themselves to move the traffic along.

Chatter continued in the background:

"…couldn't've been in her right mind, riding back there without a seat belt. Anybody see the gun?"

"…heard they were headed to Jolly Mill…"

"…woman was a doctor? Glad I never had to go to her."

"…not a dent in that big ol' grader…"

"The chief didn't hit it, silly. It was a diversion. Special kind of roadblock."

"...heard from the DOT director yet? Somebody oughta be out here...."

"Called 'em. On his way. Good thing they were doing work down here."

Finally, John spotted the sheriff knee-deep in some kind of conference with several other officers while they waited for the coroner to arrive. John would give his report shortly, but first he had something more pressing he wanted to do.

He looked down at Lynley, cuddled to his side beneath his arm, and she felt so good to him, alive, shivering just a little, but alive. "You okay, honey?" The endearment slipped out. Strange, he'd never called Sandra that.

"I'm not cold, if that's what you mean. I'm just...kind of waking up. It's all hitting me."

"I know. I'm right here." He drew her closer, reached for her head with his other hand and pulled her as near as possible, kissed her forehead with all the tenderness he felt for her at this moment. He'd thought for sure he was going to lose her—that they would lose each other, all because of one greedy, out-of-her-mind woman who couldn't handle the consequences of life's hardship.

He thought about his conversation with Lynley about solitude. But he'd meant what he said to her earlier—they wouldn't have been together every day, or spent so much time on the phone with each other every spare moment they had, if they weren't connected at the heart. In fact, he couldn't remember a time these past months when he wasn't thinking about her, or logging something in his mind to tell her later.

His excuse had been that they were the best of friends. After the scare today, he knew better.

He looked down at her, admiring her dark brown, flirty hair shining in the winter sun, eyes dark with the shock of what they'd just been through, and survived. When that deep gaze rested on him, he felt it all the way to his toes.

"I'm not happy she's dead," she said.

"No. I'm not, either. I am, however, glad to be alive. Glad you're alive. I'm also glad Gerard warned me before that big grader shot out at us."

"You mean he set this up?"

"I told him I took a defensive driving course not long ago, and I guess he thought I could handle it. He knows you well enough to know you always buckle up."

She glanced toward the crowd of firemen, policemen, the ambulance crew standing by as they waited for the coroner.

"I didn't stop suspecting Dodge until Tara shot him."

Lynley sat staring at her shoes. She'd stopped shivering. "You don't think the two of them were planning something together?"

"You're saying maybe she saw her chance to cut him out, and took it?" He patted Lynley's arm.

"Anything's possible. I was just a little...I don't know...I was incapable of believing some of those sappy things he said about me." She looked up at him.

"To be honest, if I hadn't met Dodge under suspicious circumstances, I might have found him to be a simple, harmless man who lacked maturity. He was a little...I don't know...odd. But some women might see a boyish charm in him."

"Harmless lecher, but yes. Agreed."

"I just never would have expected you to be attracted to someone like that."

She raised an eyebrow. "What kind of man would you expect me to be attracted to?"

"Someone more like...I don't know...you. Serious, responsible. Adult."

She scowled at him. "That doesn't sound nearly as sweet as those wonderful things you were saying just a few moments ago."

Okay, too late to back out of that one. "What's wrong with serious and responsible? What's wrong with being an adult? Actually, I'm kind of like that. Not, of course, that you'd ever be attracted to someone as boring and serious as—"

"Would you stop?" She laughed softly, glancing toward the men down the road. "I can't explain that wild period of my life. I was lonely in

Kansas City, and he was friendly. I'd never had a lot of attention from my father, so I guess that kind of explains why I married a clownish guy who never grew up."

"You like clowns, then." John wasn't sure he could be one.

"No. I've always hated them."

He couldn't suppress a smile. He couldn't keep from drawing her closer and relishing her touch. Her very nearness brought him peace. And hope. For the first time in years, she brought him hope.

EIGHT

Lynley felt as if her history with Dodge was a thing of strange fiction—or perhaps someone else's life. She glanced over where the coroner was now pronouncing the death of Tara Harkins, whose overly done makeup, fake red hair and revealing clothing made her look somewhat like a clown, as well. How had Lynley changed so much these past years? What on earth *had* attracted her to the man who'd lived with a prospective killer?

"I wanted a family." She said the words before she knew she was going to speak, and felt John's attention return to her. She cast a quick look up at him. "I was getting to the age when a woman starts thinking more about things like that. He was good with patients, so I figured he'd be good with kids, too." That much she had believed.

"Uh-huh." As if he couldn't quite bring himself to believe her. "And you loved him, right?"

She gave John a sharp look. Why the sudden, sarcastic tone in his voice? But she was the one who looked away first. "People love for different reasons at different times. Right now I can't say I really did love him." Now that she knew what love really was.

One more look at him told her he wasn't convinced.

"Now that I'm trying to recall it, I can't," she said. "I guess I was in love with the person I thought he was."

"I hate that he saw your innocence and used it against you."

"I allowed myself to be fooled. I guess when you live in your imagination so much, you can't tell fiction from reality."

"You needed your imagination," John said. "It provided a safe escape."

"Maybe. I didn't…behave the way many other girls behave when they don't have strong father figures. I mean, Megan and I were good girls. We earned reputations for it. Mom kept a firm hand on me. She made up for what my father lacked in parenting, so I stuck to my schoolwork and dreamed about how different my life might be someday." She noticed John's somber face. "Don't feel sorry for me, okay?"

"I don't. I'm a little frustrated. Maybe a lot frustrated. You made one mistake and you gave up on yourself. You have so much more to offer."

She continued to study his face, the light green

eyes that often had a merry twinkle in them, the amber-auburn hair, cut short. He had a firm chin.

Until recently, Lynley had believed that good-looking men had bad hearts. John, on the other hand, had both looks and goodness.

She studied John's silhouette. It was a strong, firm face. When he first moved to Jolly Mill, her friends had shoved them together at several get-togethers, dinners after church, group trips to Roaring River, before he'd asked her out on a real, honest-to-goodness date, just the two of them. And then she'd made it clear she wanted nothing more than friendship.

"You've definitely got something on your mind," John said. "Want to share?"

She felt her skin grow warm. No, she didn't ex-actly want to share her thoughts right now.

"How did you finally figure that Dodge was like your father all over again?"

Okay, that question she could answer. "A friend of mine—a true friend—had to show me what kind of a man Dodge really was. She worked in housekeeping. One day she took me to a doctor's call room and unlocked the door, and I had my eyes opened that day. The doctor and Dodge were both fired."

"I'm sorry."

She swallowed and glanced once more down the road, where the coroner had pulled as close as possible to the SUV so they could load Tara's body more easily.

The coroner got out of the car in his usual black suit, but tennis shoes revealed that he'd quickly changed.

"We'd had what I considered to be about three decent years of marriage before my eyes were opened," she told John. "We were still working in Kansas City when Mom got breast cancer, and as you heard, it was bad. I didn't know if she would make it, so I wanted to move closer to be there for her. As you could see, I didn't think my father would have it in him to nurse her back to health. Of course, I hadn't considered that he had millions of powerful green incentives."

"I don't think your father and I would have gotten along very well."

"That incident blew my subconscious theory to pieces, though I'm only just now realizing that theory."

John gave her a questioning look.

"I always thought it was difficult for attractive men to remain faithful. I'd seen so many women fawn over my father I think deep down I decided if I married a man who looked nothing like Dad, I wouldn't have to worry about any other woman wanting him."

John was silent for a moment. "Are you sure there wasn't something about Dodge that was familiar? You mentioned he liked money a little too much."

She shrugged, staring across the road into the dead field and then at the cars inching past the accident scene. That field, though. It was, indeed, as dead as her heart had once felt. But she knew the field, come spring, would burst forth with color and life again. Was it possible her heart had gone through a fallow period, and that it could change again?

"Takes a while to recover, doesn't it?" John said.

"The past now seems more like a distant dream."

"No wonder you felt as if you could never trust anyone again."

She closed her eyes, picturing these local fields in summer. "Oh, I don't know about that. There are people in my life I know I can trust." She looked up at John, and held his gaze, and let him read whatever he wanted to read.

"Um, do you think it's necessary to tell Mom about Tara's history with my father? I mean, Mom was fighting for her life and for once, Dad seemed helpful. Does she really need the memory of that time tarnished?"

"I'll try to keep that on the down-low if I can, but Lynley, I'm not sure…" He closed his eyes, obviously reluctant.

"What is it?"

"Something still doesn't feel right. I'm still wondering if Dodge was more like your father than you think."

Lynley looked up at him, and her stomach churned. "Please don't tell me you think I'm still in danger."

He held her gaze, his green eyes darkening several shades. "I think I want to go with my gut on this one."

She released a sigh, shaking away an unwanted shiver.

The Barry County sheriff came walking over. He pulled off his big cowboy hat and bowed at Lynley, then put it back on and looked at John. "Chief, you needed to see me about something a while ago, and I was buried in good-ol'-boy talk. What's up with you?"

John remained seated beside Lynley, and he didn't let her go. "I was wondering if Dodge Knowles went to the hospital, if he's okay, that kind of thing."

"I hear he's due for surgery. She got his arm pretty good, but it was a through-and-through, so he probably won't be spending time in the hospital. Why? You need to talk to him?"

"Just a few follow-up questions, but first I need to get Lynley home and collect my own vehicle. I don't think that one will be ready for a while."

"He still doesn't trust Dodge," Lynley said.

The sheriff's eyebrows disappeared under his

hat. "You think he was involved in this stuff after all?" The older man's face deepened with grooves cast by days of far too much sun and worry. "I thought we had our culprit." He jerked his head toward the hearse.

"Can't say for sure, but after a few words with the doctor friend of his, I believe she and Dodge did talk about the money she was so determined to extort. She specifically chose to stay with Dodge because he was once part of the Marshall family. I just want to see if there's any more to it than that."

The man scrunched his face. "I'll call Cassville and have an officer stop by the ER if you want to have a talk with him."

"I don't think so. I'd rather drop in unannounced."

The sheriff nodded. "Understood. Let me know if you need anything else."

As the big man walked away, Lynley looked up at John. "You sure about this? I appreciate the protection, but—"

"I'm not saying there's definitely a problem, but please? Let me do this?"

She relented only because it was impossible to miss the worry in his expression, and because it felt good to see him so concerned about covering every possibility—even the most unlikely ones.

He nudged her and nodded toward his own car,

which pulled up alongside the road out of the way of traffic. "Looks like our ride's here. You don't mind if I have a talk with Gerard about Dodge?"

She studied John's flexed jawline again. "Do what you think you must."

Lynley was waiting beside John for a break in traffic when he touched her arm. "You never told me how your father died."

"Nora Thompson killed him." She couldn't help looking up at his expression when she said it.

He frowned. "Nora?"

"That's right."

"Our own Nora Thompson? The one who practically owns half the town and was guarding Kirstie at the center today, and who makes the most delicious cookies in the four-state area?"

"Come on, John, I thought you'd read up on Jolly Mill's criminal history. It isn't extensive, but surprisingly frightening for a town our size."

"Yes, but Nora? Her record must have been expunged."

"Her act was considered self-defense. She suspected him of poisoning Mom, though we didn't know how at the time." An eighteen-wheeler blew past them, stirring debris through the air. Lynley blinked to keep the dust from her eyes. "The confrontation took place up at the rehab center before Gerard purchased it."

John looked down at her, forgetting, for a moment, about his mission to cross the road. "Why there?"

"My great-uncle Lawson Barnes owned the building at the time. Dad once worked for him, and he had a key. So did Nora. She set up a meeting to confront him about what she believed he was doing to Mom. He pulled a gun on her, and she used one of her fancy self-defense moves and pushed him over the balcony railing in the main building. She's always taking courses in cooking or self-defense. The drop was only two stories down, but you know how hard that floor is. It killed him instantly."

John whistled. "I guess you and Kirstie have good reason to trust your friends."

"We do. Mom stayed at Nora's for a few days, and started feeling better. She decided to redo the master suite, and that's when we found the mercury. After Dad was dead." Lynley shrugged. "I'm sorry I never told you. It's hard to tell a person your father was a murderer at heart."

"It doesn't change my opinion of you, though," John said.

Gerard's deep voice reached them from across the road. "Hey, you two, if you run, you might get across the road before Easter."

They walked across the street as Mom jumped out and ran to embrace Lynley. "Are you okay, honey? We can get you to the clinic and check you out."

Lynley met Megan's gaze from the passenger side in the front seat. She held her arms out to her sides. "What do you think, Doc? Do we look okay?"

"I'll do a more thorough check later." Megan glanced toward the disabled SUV. "Let's get out of here."

"Just so you know," Mom said, "I know Tara Harkins. I know what she was to your father, and—"

"And she was a pathetic woman," Lynley said with a quick, warning glance at John.

He gave her a slight nod. Mom didn't know everything, and why should she have to?

"Nothing excuses what she did," Mom said.

Lynley paused and gazed across the road at the blood-spattered SUV. She shivered at what had happened. Even worse, she couldn't help wondering what might have happened.

John opened the back door and got in first, then slid across the seat so Lynley and her mother wouldn't have to. She caught her mother's eyes and saw some grim darkness in them.

Like John, Mom wasn't convinced they were out of danger.

NINE

Lynley finished chopping a gallon of onions and was crying copiously while she poured them into a stockpot to brown before placing them over her casserole. The oven beeped. Time to stick the huge roaster inside.

"Megan? I could use some of your muscle."

Megan rinsed her gloved hands over the sink, then stripped the gloves off and stepped around the work island to open the oven door. She grabbed the other side of the pan and helped Lynley slide the bulk onto the middle rack inside.

"You seem awfully distracted this morning." She stepped back and waited for Lynley to close the industrial-size oven door.

"Can't imagine why." She couldn't stop thinking about John and his meeting today with Dodge.

"It's just a standard follow-up," Megan said, reading her mind. "The real culprit showed her true colors yesterday."

"I know, but last time John interviewed Dodge,

I was listening on my earpiece. Maybe I should've done that again."

Megan shrugged. "If you call now you might be interrupting."

Lynley looked at the huge black-and-white clock over the sink. "He's only been gone for fifteen minutes."

"Wow, girl, you do keep tabs on him."

"This is different."

"Yeah? How? You two can't stay away from each other. It wouldn't hurt to be honest with yourself for once."

Lynley grinned at her friend. "Okay, honest? I'm keeping close tabs on him right now."

"And why's that?" Megan glanced sideways at Lynley, her recently cut strawberry-blond curls quivering. "A big, tough guy like John can take care of himself. I checked him out as thoroughly as I did you, and neither of you had a single boo-boo from that accident." Her voice held a teasing lilt. "Even Kirstie's satisfied."

Lynley turned and faced her best friend since childhood. "You know how Gerard got when you were suffering from PTSD two years ago?"

Megan rolled her eyes. "I thought he'd never back off." She shrugged and grinned. "So I decided to ask him to marry me."

Lynley chuckled. "Well, that's how John's been with me. He and Mom are both still worried about me. They hover constantly. Mom had John spend the night in the guest room again last night. He slept with his loaded weapon. Mom slept with her old rifle. I slept with Data, who covered me with cat hair, but I couldn't shut him out of the room because he just kept yowling, as if he, too, is worried about me."

"Let them hover," Megan said gently. "You've been through too much. I'm worried, too."

Lynley puffed out a breath of irritability. "I wish everyone would stop treating me as if I'm breakable."

Megan gave her a one-armed hug. "I've always loved the special grace and patience you show at times like this."

"Sarcasm? Really?" Lynley picked up a long-handled spoon and stirred the onions in butter, her gaze automatically shooting to the clock.

She couldn't help remembering what John had said in front of that she-monster yesterday, about how maybe Sandra was right, after all...something like that, anyway. Hard to recall things when her heart had been racing so fast it was almost the only thing she could hear on that horrendous drive.

And then he'd said nothing about it later. So... was he just trying to distract Tara yesterday? Maybe he was sorry for what he'd said. Maybe he was having second thoughts. Maybe her honesty had messed everything up.

Megan gave her shoulder a loving slap. "Calm down and have faith that everyone around you has your best interest at heart, including John."

"I'm trying, okay?" There were just too many things to worry about. "How does one fall in love when her life might still be in danger?"

"You've been falling in love for a long time, you just wouldn't admit it," Megan said.

"How can I be sure? And what if the danger was the incentive that made John and me believe we were in love? What if we're both fooling ourselves?"

Megan's lovely eyes opened wide and her lips parted. "I'm just glad you're finally admitting it."

"We both did, but—"

"But nothing. I've been telling you for months that we need a part-time nurse down at the clinic, and I could use help up here in the infirmary. Working both places would keep you busy full-time, and you'd have no night shifts. You told me you were sick of night shifts. You know you want to be here, where John is."

"Keep in mind that no one wants to move to Jolly Mill for what they'd get paid."

"Move out of your apartment. Ask the Chief of Police to marry you, just as I drove to Texas to ask Gerard to marry me. Stay with Kirstie until you can get the wedding planned."

"I think we're moving a little too quickly."

Megan took the spoon from Lynley and took her turn at stirring. "You're right, of course. You'll make half the pay you make in Springfield."

"I have little interest in making more money than I need to live on. What good is excess money?"

Megan pulled on her gloves and returned to chopping salad. "You two have been through the fire together. Everyone in town could see what you and John couldn't."

Lynley took the caramelized onions from the heat.

"You and John have so much in common."

"Unfortunately, I think one of those things is neither of us wants to take the leap and remarry."

"I don't believe it, and neither does anyone else."

Lynley shook her head. "Words spoken under duress don't exactly make for a romantic interlude."

"You do remember the trouble I was having when Gerard came up here after me?" Megan asked.

"Of course, but you were struggling with PTSD—"

"Uh-huh, just like you are now. John's just as crazy about you as Gerard was about me."

Lynley shook her head.

Megan sighed. "You never listen."

"I want to."

Megan sank onto a kitchen chair, crossed her legs and leaned back. "Face it, you two can't stay away from each other for a full day. You talk on the phone every night when you're not together, and didn't I hear him say he'd been dropping off some of your favorite blueberry muffins when he heard you scream the other day?"

"I screamed because I'd just seen that awful note when he rang the doorbell and Data swiped against me at the same time, and just because he...you know...gave me muffins doesn't mean he plans to give me a ring, okay?"

"And he just happened to be thinking about you first thing in the morning," Megan drawled. She was developing her own version of her husband's droll sarcasm. "Ever heard of people protesting too much? I did a lot of that, myself. And don't forget, I know you too well."

Lynley's face felt a little warm. "At least Gerard's not a policeman anymore. John is, and he's the only one in town."

"I think your last excuse was that you didn't have the skills it takes to choose the right man. Gerard still places himself in danger, just as we all did this week. Life's full of danger."

"I'll never forget how you and Gerard went out of your way for us. Thank you." Oh, brother, Lynley felt her eyes tear up as if she was still chopping onions.

"You're welcome. And I deal with it because I can't imagine life without Gerard. I can't imagine you without John."

"I shouldn't have to depend on the judgment of others to choose a man." But it did help that those she trusted most approved of John. She caught herself glancing at the clock again.

"Go ahead and call him," Megan said. "You're dying to."

Lynley chuckled. "I think I'll do it outside. Watch the casserole?"

Megan shooed her out.

Lynley clipped the Bluetooth over her ear and stepped outside. She tapped it and allowed her hair to fall over it.

When he answered, she said, "Hey."

"Lynley." She closed her eyes and smiled. If she wasn't mistaken, he sounded happy to hear from her.

"Casserole's in the oven. Want me to save a plate for you?"

"Let me get this straight, you made it?"

"All by myself. It's the kitchen recipe, though. I thought I might call and eavesdrop on your conversations again today."

"Of course you did. I hate to disappoint you, but I'm not there yet. Remember, I don't drive with my foot to the floor like you do."

"I barely go over the speed limit." She decided

she had time to walk down to the house, where Mom was visiting with her best friends. Carmen Delaney seldom went anywhere these days without her Doberman, Nina, and Nora Thompson seldom traveled without a batch of her famous plate-size cookies; her most recent recipe, chocolate oatmeal, would ruin a diet faster than a full German chocolate cake.

Lynley was halfway down the hill to the house when she spied a blue car across the valley. She stopped breathing for a moment. It was parked out by the church past the edge of town.

"Lynley?"

She had to breathe again. "John." This time her voice came out in a squeak, barely more than a whisper.

"What's wrong?"

"You're not going to find the blue car at Dodge's. It's at the church again. How far away are you?"

There was a squeal of rubber on blacktop, and the roar of an engine. "I'll be there as soon as this car can get me there."

"I'll disconnect and let you focus on driving."

"No. Keep me in the loop. Don't talk, just stay on the line. Stay at the rehab center."

"But Mom's at home."

"Nora Thompson there?"

"Yes, and I'm sure Carmen brought Nina."

"Good, and if I know Nora, she'll have firepower. No one's relaxed yet after yesterday. I'll get there as soon as I can. Remember, you're the target, so stay away from that house!"

For a moment, Lynley couldn't move. She blinked and shook her head, still staring at the car. There was no denying it was the one she and John had seen yesterday at Dodge's house.

With great reluctance, she turned to walk back to the rehab center, but a dark blue shadow blocked her way, no more than thirty feet from where she stood.

She caught her breath. The person was dressed in a baggy dark hoodie like the one John had seen.

The hooded stranger turned around. It was Dodge. He looked…sly…excited. Something jutted from his right hand, and she caught the reflection of a long, sharp blade.

John flipped down his sun visor with the flashing lights and turned on his siren. If he turned left at Purdy and there were no cattle or deer in the road, he could make much better time that way than he would going up to Monett and cutting over. He edged the speed to eighty, glad for his new siren. He might get there before anything—

"Dodge." It was Lynley's soft, frightened voice.

Through the phone, he heard an indistinct male voice that grew clearer by the second. "…but we have to go see Kirstie."

"She's having a tea party, and I'm sorry, but men aren't allowed." Her voice sounded hard, angry. "Especially not men with knives."

"This won't take but a minute, honest."

John gripped the steering wheel and stomped the accelerator.

"What are you talking about?" Lynley demanded.

"Just a short transaction."

"Forget it. Stay away from me, my mother, my friends!"

And then she gasped, and John's hands froze on the wheel.

"I'm sorry." Dodge's voice sounded much darker than Lynley's. It sounded frightening. "I must insist."

"What are you going to do, knife me?" she demanded. "Then what? In seconds you'll be surrounded and arrested and you'll spend the rest of your sorry life in prison."

John's teeth ground against themselves. "Calm down, honey. I'm on my way. Play along, please! I can't lose you now."

"You know I don't want to do that." Dodge's voice grew clearer. "But I've worked on this plan for a long time, and now that you managed to stop my partner from cutting me out of the deal, I get my chance."

"You honestly think Mom still has that money? She outwitted my father years ago by making sure the money never even made it to her hands so it would never get into his."

"Yeah, and Jolly Mill is a land where everyone is sweet and filled with sunshine. Give me a break. No one gives millions of dollars away to help a bunch of strangers." The voice was different from the one that John had wanted to believe yesterday.

"What's this we have?" Dodge asked. "You're talking to someone on your earpiece? Is it John, like it was yesterday? We can't have that."

John heard a muffled cry from Lynley, and then a clatter as her earpiece fell to the ground. The line went silent.

Trying hard not to panic, John called Gerard's number, and as soon as the man picked up, he said, "Lynley's being held at knifepoint—"

"By Dodge Knowles. I know. Megan was watching her from the window. She recognized the oversize hoodie from Mrs. Drews's description the other day."

"He was working with Tara, as I'd feared. Gerard, can you get to them without being seen?"

"I'm on my way now. Where are you?"

"A lot closer than I was three minutes ago. Don't let him hurt Lynley."

"I won't let him hurt anyone. A gun has much better range than a knife."

"I can't be sure he isn't carrying another weapon, as well."

"John, just drive. Fast."

TEN

A sharp pain shot down Lynley's neck as the edge of Dodge's knife dug into her flesh.

"You don't have a choice," he snarled. "You'll enter the house like you own the place, or I'll shove you in covered in blood. Which would your mother prefer?"

"But I don't own the house. It's my mother's house. You're worse than your partner," Lynley said. "And that's saying something. There is no money."

"Oh, by the way, thank you for getting her out of my way. She got a little intrusive, wouldn't you say?"

Lynley glared over her shoulder at him, ignoring the knife. "Too bad her aim was off yesterday."

The blade dug a little more deeply. Lynley nearly fainted from the pain, and it made her angry. "The pity is that a nurse and a doctor—people who once swore oaths to do no harm—are now the ones doing the worst harm."

He shoved her forward. The upper deck door of Mom's house was barely a dozen steps away, and though Lynley was too frightened to think of words to pray, she felt prayers going up nevertheless. She continued to move as slowly as she could.

"Tell me something, Dodge. Did you really decide to marry me because my father told you about Mom's family money?"

"Let's just say it was a nice consideration."

"Of course. It wouldn't do for you to actually earn a living, would it? As long as someone else supports you, why lift a finger to help others?" If she'd been in the proper position, she'd have been tempted to spit in his face.

"Oh, stop agonizing about it. You and your new buddy'll soon be married and live your lives out schlepping for others, happy as any two country hicks can be. I'll soon have my money and we'll both be happy."

"There's no money for you." What would he do when he realized she was telling the truth?

"Tara was kind enough to set up a well-funded offshore account and give me the numbers. All I need your mother to do is send a wire to that account. No problem, and then I'll be on my way. Simple."

Lynley was close enough to look through the kitchen window, and she saw what she'd wanted to see. Carmen Delaney, one of Mom's best friends and a fellow staff member at the clinic, had brought her Doberman, Nina. They were sitting around the kitchen table.

"I should go in first." Lynley stepped around to the sliding glass door and pulled it open. She looked back at Dodge, who held the knife close while the women in the living room gasped and cried out.

There was a low growl, and then the huge black Doberman raced across the room toward her. She knew Nina was coming to greet her, but Dodge didn't.

"Keep that mutt away from me!"

Nina was a well-behaved animal. When Lynley patted her chest, the dog did as she was told and jumped up, her paws reaching Lynley's shoulders. Then she caught sight of Dodge. The playful growl became a deadly threat.

John unhooked the straps on the holster that held his .40 mm Glock, released the safety on the weapon and raced around the side of Kirstie's house, gun raised as he rushed the wooden steps to the lower deck.

A loud shout startled him from just inside the open glass door. He froze, hearing a growl he recognized as Nina's, and then stepped forward enough to see the navy blue hood that had crept into his nightmares the past two nights. Nina stood on all fours, head down, fangs bared very close to Dodge's right thigh.

John cocked his gun to announce himself, and aimed it at the navy blue hood, straight for the heart of the man wearing it. But Dodge held Lynley too closely.

He saw dark-haired Nora and blonde Carmen standing on either side of Kirstie. All three women looked ferocious. They also looked helpless.

"Your decision, Dodge," John said, knowing he couldn't shoot and risk hitting Lynley. "Nina's not happy. Neither am I, and this weapon has a hair trigger."

"I'll cut her." Dodge was no longer the friendly little man who'd been so concerned about his ex-wife's safety yesterday. Obviously, his desperation to get his hands on millions of dollars had made him quite the actor. He drew the knife back as if to plunge it forward.

Lynley jabbed her elbow up and back into his wounded shoulder.

Nina leaped up and knocked him to his knees. John kicked the knife from his hands and grabbed him by the collar, wresting him from Nina's jaws. He pressed the barrel of his weapon against the back of Dodge's head. "Give me a reason to pull this trigger."

Gerard came sprinting around the corner.

"Pat him down," John said, pulling out his cuffs.

* * *

Lynley wrapped her arms around Nina and kissed her snout. The dog wagged her stubby tail in ecstasy as Mom, Carmen and Nora surged forward.

"Time for cookies!" Nora announced, and pulled out her carrier. "I brought a chew bone for Nina."

And so the party—barely interrupted by a greedy little man who knew nothing about real wealth—picked up where it had left off.

John returned from his duties, and the women surrounded the man of the hour. John looked down at Lynley as if he never wanted to let her out of his sight again, and with everyone looking on, he took her into his arms.

"I meant what I said yesterday," he said quietly in her ear.

Lynley smiled up at him. "Sandra would approve?"

"I approve." He drew her away from the crush of the happy partiers. She grabbed a cookie on the way out the door behind him.

She broke it, took a bite of her half, and gave him the other half. "Celebrate?"

He bit into his half, eyes never leaving hers until they closed with abandon.

"Think Sandra would approve of that for a wedding cake?" Lynley asked.

Suddenly mortified, she realized what she'd said. She'd just asked him to marry her.

Nearly choking on cookie crumbs, she walked to the edge of the deck and nuzzled Data, who had been banished outside so Nina wouldn't mistake him for a party favor.

John stepped up behind her. "From now on, Sandy isn't the one I need to please," he said, his voice gentle but serious.

Lynley turned and looked up at him.

"I'm moving forward. You're helping me, Lynley Marshall. Or maybe we could make that Lynley Russell."

She grinned, nodded, speechless.

He took both their cookies into his hand and wrapped his free arm around her. He drew her up against him and kissed her. He tasted of spice and chocolate, and the feeling was delicious in every way.

"My dream come true," she said, smiling up at him. "You'll never know how happy I was to see you arrive."

"And you'll never know how happy I was to get here in time. I might've burned out the motor in my car, but you're worth far more than a million car motors." As if unable to prevent himself, he kissed her again, and drew her close once more.

"I think I've learned a lot these past years," Lynley said as she glanced at the women hovering by the sliding glass door, shamelessly watching the two of them and cheering, toasting with cups of tea and cookies. She saw John had noticed them, too.

"I think they have something in mind," he said.

"What on earth could that be?"

He drew her down the steps and around the house for a little privacy. They sat down together on the porch swing. "I think they hear wedding bells."

So did she.

John laughed and handed her back her half of the cookie. "I'm ready to try again."

She kissed his chin. "So am I." She never thought she'd say that.

"There'll be work to do. I want premarital counseling," he said. "I fully believe in counseling before marriage so there will be fewer bumps afterward."

Before she could say another word, he put his arms around her and drew her head to his. His kiss filled her heart and soul with healing and joy and a strange desire to ask this man, who had been determined to never marry again, if he would marry her before the next New Year came around.

And so she did.

He chuckled and drew her close, looked deeply into her eyes, dug his fingers through his hair. "How did you know what I was thinking? I love you, Lynley. You know that, don't you? I've tried every way possible to show you that these past few days."

As they kissed again on the porch swing, they grew aware that her mother's party had moved and were watching them with dreamy-looking eyes— the eyes of hopeful love.

This was exactly as it should be. Lynley sent up a silent prayer. *You knew all along, didn't You?*

It seemed His answer came in the faces of those who cared the most.

John hadn't let anyone down. Not God. Not Sandra. Not himself. It was all as it should be. God's timing was perfect.

* * * * *

Dear Reader,

John and Lynley, the characters in this novella, both struggle with issues about reconnecting on a romantic level after experiences from their pasts— John, because of his beloved wife's death; Lynley, because she chose a bad person the first time. I see great wisdom in their reluctance to make quick decisions the second time around. I've seen too many friends get their hearts broken when they jumped into a new relationship immediately following a breakup. Often, that need to be in love— no matter whom it's with—is a death knell to a second romance.

A broken romance is a devastation, and those who have had their hearts broken will never be the same. They can, however, dig deeply and learn how to make the next time a good one. It takes time. Give that gift to yourself.

I hope you've enjoyed our stories set in Jolly Mill. It's a lovely place worthy of stories. We will miss it as we move forward to new places and meet new people.

Please keep in touch with us at www.hannah-alexander.com.

Hannah Alexander

Questions for Discussion

1. I love to dream about what I'd do if I received a million dollars without the taxes to go with it. What about you?

2. In *Alive After New Year*, we see how desperate some people can become to get their hands on someone else's money. What lengths do you think you'd go to if you saw an opportunity?

3. Have you ever had something others wanted so badly they would pretend to befriend you in order to get what you had?

4. Do you find yourself resenting those you perceive to be wealthier than you? Why or why not?

5. False perceptions can cause a lot of trouble. How many people who live in big houses and drive expensive cars do you believe truly can afford what they have?

6. Kirstie Marshall willingly refused the wealth that could have been hers when she realized her husband might be killing her to get his hands on it. Do you think she's the kind of person who might give it all away, anyway?

7. Lynley insisted on returning home to help her mother when she developed a deadly form of breast cancer. Did she break the biblical rule to "leave and cleave"?

8. If you'd been Lynley when Dodge remarked about how wealthy they could become if Kirstie died, what would your reaction have been?

NEW YEAR'S TARGET

Jill Elizabeth Nelson

To the love of my life who couldn't be more
my opposite or more dear to me.
Without the Lord as our glue, we might never have
taken a second look at each other.

To the staff at the many fine apartment facilities
who, like me, take pride in providing
quality housing at an affordable price.

O Lord, You have heard the desire and the longing
of the humble and oppressed;
You will prepare and strengthen and direct their hearts;
You will cause Your ear to hear,
To do justice to the fatherless and oppressed,
So that man, who is of the earth,
May not terrify them any more.
—*Psalms* 10:17–18

ONE

Cassidy Ferris grinned into the chill rush. Her exposed teeth might be cold enough to shatter by the time she reached the bottom of the slope, but the ski runs offered the only pleasure she was likely to find during this entire nightmare of a New Year's weekend. How had she let her cousins talk her into such a thinly disguised attempt to match her up with her soul mate during this "Weekend of Romance and Inspiration" at the Aspen Grand Ski Lodge?

At least she could enjoy the skiing part. Cassidy tossed her head and laughed. Her muscles sang, the wind scoured her cheeks and the rays of the newly risen sun shot sparks from the crystalline snow—like gliding through a shower of light.

Zigzag stemming brought her to the edge of the run, and she changed trajectories. A bank of pine trees loomed on her left. She offered them ample berth. A lone aspen stabbed the air to her right, easy to avoid. Smooth sailing! She'd reach the bottom in record t—

A stunning force burned across the back of her head.

The oblique blow sent her into a stumble. One speeding ski made an X with the other, and in a split instant, she tumbled top over tail. Her head and shoulders slammed against the stand-alone tree. Air gushed from her chest, and her bones rattled. She lay on her side, brain ping-ponging in her skull. Her lungs sucked in vain for a precious molecule of oxygen.

Light narrowed to a glistening pinpoint, then at last she managed a tiny breath of air and her vision returned. A figure loomed over her. Cassidy squinted upward. Only one other person had braved the ski slopes this early in the morning. She'd spotted him, clad in a red jacket with a horizontal black strip across the chest, striding toward the registration cabin just as she boarded the lift to ride to the top of the advanced slope.

This guy wore that jacket. Had he run into her from behind? But why would a collision make the back of her scalp feel as if someone had laid a hot poker across her flesh? An awful suspicion formed even as liquid warmth enveloped the area.

"Are you all right?" a deep voice asked.

What was familiar in the timbre of his words? The man lifted his goggles to the top of his red stocking cap and peered down at her with a pair of eyes that rivaled a mountain meadow for green intensity. Cassidy lost what little air her quivering lungs had managed to drag in.

What cruel joke dictated that the last person she ever wanted to see now reached out a gloved hand to touch her cheek? If she could move, she'd never let Tim Halstead lay so much as a pinky on her.

Was he her assailant? Might be a nice, neat explanation, but he had to have been skiing down the mountain behind her. No way could he have fired a bullet that drew a straight line across the back of her neck. That meant a shooter was still out there and might pull the trigger again. She rolled her eyes to the right and left, but spotted no one. The pine grove was the only place a sniper could hide, and every second that passed with Tim and her out in the open increased the opportunity for another shot—lethal this time.

"Get down," she snarled.

"What?" Tim's square jaw slackened.

"We need to take cover as best we can behind this tree."

"Take it easy. You've had a bad tumble." He lifted both hands in a gesture designed to placate hysteria. "I'll call for help."

Her archenemy from her teenage years was as oblivious and contrary as ever. She was going to have to take action and force them both into cover whether she felt capable of movement or not. Gathering her reluctant muscles, she lunged for Tim's legs. Behind her, something snapped. A tree branch? No time to look over her shoulder. With a satisfying yelp, her target toppled sideways, and they both rolled into the shadow of the aspen and down several feet behind a small snowdrift.

Cassidy landed on her side, minus one ski. The other stabbed kitty-corner into the snow. She kicked loose and turned toward Tim, who sprawled on his back, legs splayed, and the backs of both skis rammed deeply into the snow crust.

"What on God's great earth did you do that for?" Steam heated every word, but the response was out of character. The Tim she'd known in high school would have boiled the air with curses.

Cassidy ripped the goggles from her face, taking her olive-green stocking cap with them. She examined the back of the cap and sucked in a brisk breath between her teeth. Suspicion confirmed. A pair of holes bookended a wide line darkened with blood. A streak of unraveled knitting connected the entrance and exit holes.

Her would-be rescuer was struggling toward a sitting position.

"Stay down," she hissed and rolled over on her stomach, ignoring warm trickles down the back of her neck.

Cassidy poked her head over the drift just high

enough to gain a view of the row of pine trees about fifty yards distant. She blinked and squinted, but the trees wouldn't stop jigging around in her woozy vision. What made her think she might be able to spot a sniper if she couldn't see straight? And why had she not heard the report of the rifle? Were they dealing with a professional using a silencer? If so, the gunman was either long gone, or he lay in wait for her to expose herself to another shot.

Either way, she was in no shape to defend herself—much less anyone else. Who could possibly have guessed she'd need her sidearm for a holiday getaway?

A fresh burst of pain erupted in her skull. With a groan, she rolled over and curled into a fetal ball with a mitten-clad hand pressed against the wound. *Breathe. Just breathe.* Now would not be an opportune time to lose consciousness...or give up the remnants of the bagel she'd scarfed down for breakfast. Her stomach rolled ominously.

"Lay still. I'm making that call." Her companion pulled a cell phone from his jacket pocket and started to stand up.

"What part of stay down don't you understand?" She lifted her pounding head and glared at him. "We're in danger."

She thrust the telltale stocking cap toward him,

but he just gaped at her from a frozen-in-place half squat.

"Cassidy Ferris?"

Jelly beans for him! He recognized the gangly misfit from their high school days. But then, why wouldn't she occupy at least a footnote in the "memorable clown" category after the mean stunt he pulled on her at their junior prom? *Her* junior prom, anyway. He'd been a senior. Cassidy never went to her senior prom—for a reason more terrible than personal humiliation.

No time for reliving the bad old days.

"Look at the cap and then make that call. Or better yet, the other way around." Cassidy slumped back, resting the heat of her wound against the cool snow. Crazy-making bees buzzed in her head. Good thing Tim had his cell phone with him. Hers was charging on the bedside table at the lodge.

The rescue crew had better get here quickly. Whoever had tried to take her out would find them as sitting ducks…if he were still around. Of all the feelings in the world, she hated helplessness the most. Maybe that's why she chose the career she did. The Halsteads—father and sons—had played a big role in setting her course for life, and now she was stuck depending on one of them in a deadly situation.

God, You sure have a quirky sense of humor.

"You've been shot!" cried her unwelcome companion. "A bullet did this." Eyes wide, he lifted the stocking cap, torn bit splayed across his fingers.

"Ya think, Sherlock?" she muttered as darkness squeezed her consciousness into oblivion.

Tim stared at the woman sprawled in the snow. Cassidy Ferris. What were the odds that he'd run into—almost literally—his most cherished nightmare here on the Aspen slopes?

A narrow trickle of red snaked from beneath the wealth of black hair that was escaping a ponytail. All color had leached from her skin. If not for the midnight lashes and brows and the frame of ebony hair, her face would have blended in with the snow.

He shook the damaged stocking cap off his hand and made that 9-1-1 call, even as he scanned their surroundings for any sign of a gunman. "And you'd better send the police, as well. This is not a common skiing accident. She's been shot."

"Shot, sir?" The dispatcher's voice sharpened. "Are you sure?"

Tim glared at the damaged cap. "I'm sure."

He pocketed his phone and elbow-crawled up to the verge of the snowdrift. Nothing but white powder and that strip of pine trees. Unless…Tim narrowed his eyes on a dark spot moving across a distant ridge. If only he had binoculars. Either a bear standing on its hind legs was slogging its way over the top, or a person on snowshoes was making pretty good time away from them.

How had Cassidy Ferris drawn the ire of a killer? The woman could goad a monk into a tantrum—and he'd been anything but sanctified back in their high school days. So much had changed for him since then, but she wouldn't know that.

Tim pulled back and hunkered down by Cassidy. He touched her throat and found the pulse strong and steady. She always was a tough one. The thin worm of red on the white snow had not lengthened or widened, so the bleeding must have stopped. But who knew what damage that bullet had done to such a fine mind, though she'd seemed pretty sharp until she lost consciousness.

"Hang in there, Cass."

He smiled grimly. That famous temper would be riled but good if she heard the likes of him using the abbreviation of her name reserved for close friends and family.

She let out a low groan and opened her eyes. Tim's gut tightened. Amazing. The unusual amber color had deepened with the passage of nearly a decade since last he'd seen her. She began to wriggle into a sitting position.

"Don't move!" he ordered. "Help is on the way."

"I'm fine!"

"People don't pass out when they are fine. You've been shot in the head. You—"

"A flesh wound. Slamming into that tree did more damage. Probably some degree of concussion."

Tim jerked his brows together. "What are you, a doctor?"

She didn't answer as she levered herself into a sitting position. Stubborn woman. His hands itched to help her, but he'd no doubt be belted for his effort. Not slapped. Cassidy was the slugging, not the slapping, type.

"No sign of the shooter?" Her gaze examined him.

He told her about the retreating speck on the horizon.

"Did you hear the shot?"

"Nothing but the swoosh of my skis and the wind in my ears."

"Same here." Her generous lips thinned. "Help me get to that band of pine trees. I want to check out the gunner's nest. He was bound to leave evidence behind."

"Are you nuts? Let the cops handle that."

"I *am* a cop."

"Oh."

Amusement flickered in those extraordinary eyes.

A whole row of tumblers clicked into place in Tim's new impression of this old nemesis. Cassidy, a cop? Of course. The career choice fit with her get-the-bad-guy-and-make-him-pay personality, as well as her natural athleticism.

He crossed his arms. "I'm not helping you move, except onto a stretcher. You're going to the hospital. You may be a cop somewhere, but I'll bet you've got no jurisdiction here."

"Seattle."

"You never left the hometown?"

"I'm still around…and in position to be a real burr under Halstead Enterprises' saddle. But I'm sure you know all about that. Enjoyed a run-in with Trace a few weeks ago. Didn't he give you my regards?"

Tim's insides turned to stone as their gazes dueled.

"My office is in California. Trace and I don't see much of each other."

Her sudden blink betrayed surprise. Tim hid a grin. *Gotcha!* Such moments were rare as golden hen's teeth with this female. A sour taste invaded his mouth. Disliking her would be less bothersome if he didn't find her so admirable…not to mention attractive.

Conversation stalled, but their gazes seemed welded together. Cassidy had always been striking, and she'd grown more so with the passing years. *Cute* was not a word anyone would apply to this woman. But then, cute had never interested him.

When they were in school together, a lot of the guys had found her intimidating and enticing at the same time, a weird combination that made adolescent males act out with defensive aggression. At least that's how he'd explained the phenomenon to himself in the years since graduation. Or maybe the problem was that he still hadn't figured out which he wanted to do more—kiss Cassidy Ferris or strangle her.

Unfortunately—or maybe fortunately, depending on one's outlook—she'd never returned the interest. Far from it. Halsteads were dog meat in her books, and sadly enough, he couldn't blame her for the opinion.

"So what have you been doing since last we met?" she said.

"Graduated from law school a couple of years ago. Passed the bar, and now I'm—"

"Working for Halstead Enterprises. I'm sure your father can always use legal services. What better representation could he get than his own son?"

The cheery tone emphasized the contempt behind the words. But it wasn't the attitude toward Halstead Enterprises that jabbed like an ice pick; it was the assumption that he'd go into business defending the company. He'd sooner spend the rest of his life slinging hash in a greasy spoon—

as he'd done in college—than work with his father and brother.

He opened his mouth and then shut it. Forget trying to explain. Words wouldn't mean much to Cassidy. Let her think what she would. She'd do that with or without his permission.

The *whump-whump* of a helicopter drew their attention skyward. The chopper sported a giant-size Red Cross logo on its side. Quick response, though it had seemed a slice of eternity.

Tim rose and took a step toward the whirlybird settling down in a cloud of white at the bottom of the run. Tingles pebbled his flesh as he exposed himself in the open, even though it was reasonable to suppose the shooter had gone.

A rustle of nylon fabric told him Cassidy had stirred. He looked over his shoulder to find her standing up, but leaning against the lone tree. He'd forgotten how tall she was, a good inch over his six-one. Not that he'd ever minded her slight height advantage. He couldn't say the same for his male classmates—his brother Trace, in particular.

Tim winced at a flare of memory from his senior prom. Cassidy would probably be stunned to know that the foolish incident was the defining moment that set his life on a trajectory away from his birth family. The senseless tragedy that occurred a year later drove the wedge deep and wide.

A couple of medics wearing Red Cross logo

jackets piled out of the helicopter. Tim waved to them. On their heels, a burly figure descended. A ray of the morning sun shot spangles from a bit of metal on the left breast of his jacket—the local sheriff.

He glanced at Cassidy. The out-thrust jaw and hard stare spoke loud and clear. The only way for the shooter to stop Cassidy from tracking him down would be to kill her.

He could opt to keep his distance from the situation, but his family owed her family big-time in a way that money could never repay. Dad and Trace sneered at their culpability. Apparently, he was the only Halstead with a conscience. Maybe God had thrown him into this situation to do whatever he could to save a Ferris.

Big problem, Lord. He rolled his eyes heavenward. *I have no idea how I could possibly help Cass in a way that she can't do for herself.*

Law school didn't provide training in confronting murderers anywhere but in the safety of the courtroom, much less in curbing the reckless courage of a woman like Cassidy Ferris. Nevertheless, he'd have to accept the assignment and succeed— or die trying. With a killer on the loose, that saying might be more than a cliché.

TWO

No way would Cassidy heed the doctor's recommendation and spend an overnight under observation in the hospital. Truthfully, she wasn't as steady as she put on, and pain slithered around the edges of her brain. However, hunkering down in a hospital room with one egress didn't sit well with the itchy target painted between her shoulder blades.

Exiting the exam area, she halted on the threshold to the waiting room, senses on high alert for anything "off." Her attacker could easily figure out she'd be taken to the nearest ER, but it was hard to believe he'd hang out here waiting for another chance in front of so many witnesses.

Cassidy's gaze roamed, then backtracked onto an unwelcome presence seated near the wall with one ankle propped across the opposite knee. Engrossed in an outdoor sports magazine, Tim was probably the most relaxed person in the area. Divested of his snow pants and jacket, which sat in a chair next to him, casual attire of jeans and long-sleeve, button-down shirt left no doubt that he'd retained his offensive tackle physique since his high school glory days.

Why was Tim Halstead here? Sure, the sheriff had ordered him into town with her to give a statement to a deputy, but that didn't mean Tim needed to check on her. She could ignore him, sneak away without him seeing her, but avoidance wasn't in her nature. Even when it might be in her best interest.

She marched over to Tim. "Hasn't anyone told you that you're free to return to the lodge? You could be boarding or skiing instead of just reading about it."

His gaze lifted from the magazine. "A, I just got done giving my statement to a deputy who, by the way, is lurking around waiting to talk to you. B, the next bus back to the lodge doesn't leave for an hour and a half. And C, don't pass out again, but I wanted to find out how you're doing. They aren't keeping you?" He scanned her up and down.

Cassidy clenched her fingers against the urge to make a futile attempt at smoothing her hair into place. From the exam room mirror, she was well aware that she resembled a black-haired Little Orphan Annie who'd stuck her finger into an electrical socket—except where the bullet had ripped the hair from the nape of her neck. The shaving process around that spot, prior to the application of a bandage, had cost her another hunk and hadn't done her coiffure any favors. At least her skull wasn't mummy-swathed.

Who cared how Tim Halstead regarded her anyway? She didn't. *Yeah, right.* If only she'd applied a little makeup this morning. Not the hour's worth of primping her twin cousins, Dacy and Daria, performed day in and day out, but why, oh why, couldn't she have spared ten minutes to highlight her femininity? This was one of the things she hated most about Tim Halstead. He made her long to be pretty. At least, seeing admiration in his eyes would add a great deal of satisfaction to spurning him.

"Earth to Cassidy."

She blinked at Tim's verbal nudge. *Great!* Now she was space case du jour.

Cassidy cleared her throat. "I have strict instructions to refrain from activities that contain risk of hitting my head again, but I'm not required to stay."

"Translation—you refused. Is that wise?" He laid his magazine aside and rose.

Their comparable heights put them eye to eye.

"Since when have I chosen caution over necessary action?"

A sudden grin displayed the dimple in his left

cheek that made Tim a devastating cross between boy next door and forbidden heartthrob.

"Since never," he said. "But I could argue that 'necessary action' might be better served if you allowed yourself recuperation time."

"Who says I'm not going to take it easy?"

Tim lifted a brow.

"For the rest of the day anyway."

The other brow lifted.

Further retort stuck on her tongue. Of course, she might retire to her room at the lodge, but she'd be racking her aching brain about anyone who might have a vendetta against her. Then she'd be on the phone with her partner back at the precinct to follow up on her ideas. Maybe she was a little driven. Just a little.

"All right. You've got me. How about I promise to take a nap?"

Why was she promising Tim Halstead anything—as if she could believe he cared? But she didn't seem able to control her blathering mouth... or the illogical desire to please him. Wasn't she forgetting someone she'd promised never to forget? Shame burned through her.

Francine, I'm sorry. You deserve better than me wasting time with a Halstead. Even if said Halstead did call 9-1-1 when Cassidy was in a bind, his action preserved his own skin as much as hers, considering there was a sniper who might have been as interested in taking out a witness as in eliminating his target.

Cassidy snapped her jaw shut, turned and nearly rammed into the burly chest of a short man with thick, graying hair who wore a deputy sheriff's badge. At the sudden halt, pain stabbed through her skull and she saw stars.

"Cassidy Ferris?" the deputy asked.

"You got me."

"I'm Deputy Stewart Blaine of the Pitkin County Sherriff's Office. I need to ask you some questions."

"I have a few for you also. Particularly about any findings at the crime scene."

Deputy Blaine pursed his lips, and unless Cassidy missed her guess, barely suppressed an eye roll. "We will keep you as informed as we can, Miss—"

"Detective. It's Detective Junior Grade Cassidy Ferris of Seattle PD's West Precinct."

The deputy's eyes narrowed, his lips thinned and a predatory gleam entered his mud-brown gaze. Cops hated cop killers—or attempted cop killers—even if they didn't serve on the same force.

"Call me Stew," he said. "Let's go grab coffee in the cafeteria. You can fill me in on your thoughts and observations."

"Sounds like a plan. I'm Cass to my colleagues."

Ignoring the slight pull on her head bandage, she glanced over her shoulder at Tim. "Feel free to take the next bus back to the lodge."

Tim scowled and crossed his arms. "Coffee? I'm sure the doctor will be delighted to hear you're imbibing caffeine after a head injury."

Cassidy planted her hands on her hips. "*You're* a physician now...? Never mind. Haven't you heard of decaf?"

"Heard of it." Tim's lips formed a thin smirk. "Not sure you intended to drink it until I got in your face. But pay me no attention. It's none of my business if you pass out, hit the floor and aggravate your concussion. Maybe then you'll get some bed rest."

"This your boyfriend?" the deputy asked.

"No!"

The word burst from Cassidy and Tim in chorus.

"Coulda fooled me." Stewart chuckled then sobered as she fixed him with a glare.

Turning her back on her chief irritation, Cassidy smoothed her expression. "Kindly lead the way. I'm new around here."

Stewart started up a hallway, and Cassidy followed, at last breathing air free from Halstead presence. A small sound from behind alerted her, and she spared a sidelong glance to their rear. Did the guy never get a hint?

She turned toward their not-so-subtle tail. "We can't allow you to take part in this conversation."

Tim gazed at her with a bland expression. "Converse away. Call in the FBI for all I care. I'm after a cup of coffee—full strength—and a sandwich. I have time to kill before that bus ferries me back up the mountain. Oh, and you're losing your escort." He motioned up the hallway.

Cassidy swiveled just in time to see the deputy turn a corner. Without another word, she left Tim in her wake. If ever a more aggravating man were created on the face of this planet, she'd yet to meet him.

Tim grinned after Cassidy's retreating back then yanked his lips into sobriety. What kind of creep got a kick out of riling an injured woman? More of the *old* Halstead persona must linger inside him than he'd thought. Then again, his breath had always been swept away when Cassidy morphed into that magnificent eagle with ruffled feathers.

The lunchroom was mostly vacant, but he spotted Cassidy and Deputy Blaine at the coffee machine. He wasn't close enough to see if she had chosen decaf. Not that he really cared. *Yep, way to lie to yourself.* Maybe over the years he'd successfully buried his mixed-up adolescent feelings for her, but one look into those amber eyes had resurrected them with stunning ferocity.

Frowning, he selected a couple of slices of rye bread and began constructing his lunch from the sandwich bar. He needed to get a mature handle on these emotions she stirred. He had no hope for reciprocation of interest—not after the part his family played in the tragedy with her cousin Francine—so he might as well turn off his attraction meter now.

Tim finished making his sandwich and grabbed a caffeinated soda then found a secluded table and settled in. At least Cassidy couldn't accuse him of choosing a seat for the purpose of eavesdropping. She and the deputy hadn't even sat down yet.

A few minutes later, familiar voices coming from the other side of a nearby pillar halted the second half of his sandwich on its way to his mouth. Maybe he should let them know they'd chosen a spot a few feet from him. *Nah!* He was here first. Let them talk. It wasn't his fault if he found out something useful to his rather absurd objective of protecting Cassidy. He needed all the advantage he could get when tilting at windmills.

"It's reasonable to suspect that the shooter has a vendetta against me from one of my cases," Cassidy said. "I'll get my partner in Seattle to dig around for who in my case history might recently have been released from prison."

"Or a relative of someone who's still behind bars," Blaine said.

"Good thinking."

The deputy snorted. "Somebody has to be awfully determined if they followed you to Aspen. You ever kill someone in the line of duty or help send someone up for life or lethal injection?"

"Negative. Though I did have cause to fire my weapon a month or so ago. A couple of meth tweekers jumped my partner and me in a supposedly abandoned house. They were out of their skulls. Even my Taser didn't faze the brute I tangled with. When he came after me with a fireplace poker, I had to shoot. He lived, but I spent a week on desk duty until Internal Affairs cleared me on the use of deadly force."

Tim sat transfixed as a mental image of Cassidy accosted by a crazed meth head played through his imagination. His gut twisted, and he laid the remains of his sandwich on his plate. From the inflection of her voice, the most harrowing part of the incident was the desk duty.

"Who's this Tim Halstead to you?" Blaine's tone sharpened. "He anybody we should be looking at? When I interviewed him, he didn't mention knowing you, but from what I saw in the waiting room, you two have a history."

Hairs at the base of Tim's neck prickled. How would Cassidy respond to that bald question? A blistering tirade? Her bright laugh was the last thing he expected.

"I knew the guy in high school. Had no idea he was going to attend this New Year's bash at the lodge, which makes it interesting running into him hundreds of miles from home. I see red flags about the coincidence, but Tim's in the clear as far as being the shooter."

Good. At least she thought better of him than to suspect him of attempted murder. He was a little puzzled over the coincidental meeting element, too, but stranger things had happened. Tim's appetite returned, and he picked up his sandwich.

"He arrived at the slope *after* I did," Cassidy continued. "The bullet caught me horizontally across the back of my skull. I can probably thank a sudden change of skiing trajectory for that little mercy. The stand of pine trees is the only place where the shot could have originated, and Tim couldn't have gotten there ahead of me."

He scowled at his ham and cheese. Her dismissal of him as the attempted murderer had nothing to do with some redeeming quality she saw in his character. What had he expected?

"I can verify that's where the sniper hid," Blaine said. "The sheriff called me before I caught up with you here. They found a spot where someone knelt in the snow and there were snowshoe tracks in and out. The tracks intersect with an old logging road a couple of ridges away. We got tread marks so maybe we can match them with a vehicle type."

"Old logging road? Then we're looking for someone familiar with the area?"

The deputy barked a laugh. "Or anyone who bought one of those fancy tourist maps that marks everything but the deer tracks."

Cassidy's sigh conveyed a wealth of disgust. "Not much of a lead then. Were there any shell casings?"

"Nope."

"Careful killer. Must've gathered them up."

"Them?"

"I think he took a second shot. I heard wood snap behind me when I knocked Tim off the side of that snowdrift. Your forensics team didn't find a bullet embedded in the aspen tree by any chance?"

"Forensics *team?* Up here in the boonies we've got one forensics officer. The rest of us pinch-hit under his direction. Good lead, though. I'll call it in."

"Do that. Thanks. I'd better head out to catch the bus. I may pack up my stuff and leave for home. The sooner I'm behind a badge with a side-arm strapped on, the better. Besides, I'd hate for anybody else to get hurt if the killer makes another attempt at that crowded lodge."

Sounds of chair legs scraping against the floor punctuated the comments. Footsteps trod away. Tim waited thirty seconds then ditched the re-mainder of his sandwich and headed out of the hospital. It was a free country. If he wanted to keep a weather eye on Cassidy's back, she couldn't stop him. Besides, he needed to go to the bus stop, too.

Brisk air scrubbed his cheeks as he halted on the sidewalk to zip up his winter jacket. He gazed around the parking lot and across the snowy cityscape. How had Cassidy disappeared so quickly? There was no sign of her in any direction. Maybe she used another exit. Or maybe Deputy Blaine gave her a ride.

Expelling a puff of frost-white air, Tim headed toward the bus stop. What could he do about it if Cassidy broke her word about getting some rest and took right off for Seattle? Not a thing.

He'd probably go home himself—San Francisco, not Seattle. The luster had worn off this impromptu vacation. How *had* he been enticed into attending this event? A well-meaning buddy, of course, who was trying to help him get over his recent breakup with Luca, his long-term girlfriend. Not much of a breakup. More like a drift-apart. But his friends seemed to think he must be devastated, which led to them badgering him to go along on this trip in search of the woman of his dreams. But then the buddy ditched him for a new girlfriend who wanted him to stay in San Fran for New Year's Eve. Maybe Tim should rethink his friends.

Tim arrived at the bus stop, scowling. Several people stood in the glass-enclosed shelter, hunch-shouldered and stamping their feet against the cold. Tim checked his watch. The bus would come in ten minutes.

About half that time later, a sheriff's car pulled over on the opposite side of the road, and Cassidy climbed out the passenger side. Looking both ways up and down the semi-busy street, she jaywalked toward the bus stop, hands punched deep into her jacket pockets. The wind reddened her cheeks, but the rest of her exposed skin was as white as the proverbial sheet. Was she starting to regret not accepting a cozy berth in a hospital room?

Tim glowered and crossed his arms. Mule-headed woman!

Just as Cassidy reached the middle of the road, a screech of tires announced a vehicle flying around the corner. The car accelerated toward the pedestrian amid a chorus of screams and shouts from the observers in the bus stop shelter.

A yell sprang from Tim's throat, but there was nothing he could do.

THREE

At the screech of tires, Cassidy jumped backward, scrambled for balance on an ice patch, lost the fight, fell and rolled like a toppled bowling pin. Tires whooshed past, inches from her head. Exhaust smell blasted into her nostrils. Then the world went silent.

She lay flat on her back on hard tarmac, staring into a cloud-wisped sky, head pounding fit to burst, and thanking God for her cop-trained reflexes. Footsteps converged, and then someone knelt beside her. A face inserted itself into her woozy vision. Tim! Her stalled heart jump-started.

"Cassidy! Oh, Cass, are you all right?" The look in his eyes—terror and fury and passionate concern—injected strength into her limbs. The guy cared. Why?

"I'm all right." She struggled onto her elbows. "The car missed me…barely."

Tim's arm came around her, and he drew her close. The offered strength of a shoulder to lean on melted the edges of a frozen place deep inside. She snuggled. Other figures crowded around, voices intruding.

What was she doing in Tim Halstead's embrace?

Sitting up, she removed herself from his arms. "Either a reckless driver is tearing around Aspen, or someone targeted me again." She scanned the small crowd gaping down at her. "Did anyone get a license plate number?"

Heads shook to a chorus of "Nos" and "Sorrys" and conflicting descriptions of the vehicle.

"Was the driver male or female?" Cassidy asked.

"Male," some voices responded.

"Female," others cried.

Typical witness discrepancies in a crisis situation. Mentally shaking her head, Cassidy struggled to her feet.

Tim helped her up with a firm grip on her elbow. "The driver wore a stocking cap and sunglasses and kept his chin ducked low," he said in her ear, "but in my estimation, the breadth of the shoulders indicated a male."

"Lawyering must teach you attention to detail," she said.

She hadn't meant the remark as a sneer, but Tim must have taken it that way. He backed off to the edge of the onlookers, his expression closed. Vehicles were slowing for the pedestrians in the street. A few impatient drivers hit their horns.

Best move this party off the street and make another 9-1-1 call. She'd have Tim make the call, anyway. This day had provided a hard lesson about keeping her cell phone charged and on her at all times.

An hour later, statements given, Stewart dropped both her and Tim off in front of the imposing entrance of the Aspen Grand Lodge.

"Tonight sometime, I'll bring that item you requested and give you an update on the case," the deputy said to Cassidy as she slid out of the passenger seat.

"The sooner, the better." She waved and closed the door.

The lodge's genuine log exterior and high-end mullioned windows must have cost a fortune, as had the interior of hardwood floors, log pillars, Tiffany lamps and luxury-rustic room furnishings. Right now, she didn't care if all she found was a lumpy cot. Exhaustion hung like an anchor around her neck.

She trod up the porch stairs alongside Tim, who kept shooting glances her way. He'd been strangely quiet, hunched in the backseat, during the drive out to the lodge.

"Do you have anything to take for that headache that's digging furrows in your brow?" he asked.

She nodded. "I stopped at the pharmacy for a prescription before Stew took me to the bus stop."

Tim sucked in an audible breath. "That means whoever drove the car that almost hit you was aware of your movements. Either he followed you from the hospital or was lying in wait around the corner."

They halted and faced each other.

"We weren't followed," Cassidy clipped out.

"The alternative is scarier. He knew where you'd be going—anticipated your movements."

"Or made a lucky guess."

"Do you believe that?"

"No."

The double front doors flung wide, and a pair of feminine squeals rippled the air.

"Cass!" cried one voice.

"You're okay!" trilled the other.

A pair of petite dynamos converged on her and swept her into a group hug. For the first time since the shooting incident, Cassidy enjoyed a sense of safety. Illusion, of course, but welcome all the same.

"Dacy…Daria…am I glad to see you two."

Stepping back, Dacy's frank gaze assessed her. "We heard you'd been hurt on the ski slope."

"We were about to head down the mountain to find you." Daria left one arm around Cassidy, drawing her forward.

Cassidy looked around for Tim, but he'd disappeared. Self-preservation, no doubt. The Ferris twins would have cut him no slack, especially since they didn't know he'd been helpful to their injured cousin. And three Ferrises to one Halstead were fatal odds. Retreat was the act of a sensible man.

"Nobody seemed to know where you were taken." Dacy flopped her arms against her sides as they entered the warmth of the cavernous lobby. "The local hospital? Flown out elsewhere? How badly you were hurt? Nothing!"

"Maddening!" Daria confirmed. "What happened, anyway? The staff were, like, totally close-mouthed, but the advanced slope was off-limits for most of the morning."

Cassidy studied her cousins and sighed internally. Mirror images of lush, dusky hair, doll-baby features and blue-gray eyes brimming with bright intensity, they wore designer jeans and silky shirts that made them look elegant and fragile, but she knew them to be tougher than a pair of steel-toed boots and tenacious as terriers. She loved them to pieces, and normally she could more than keep up with their energy, but right now, collapse was imminent.

"Let me lie down, and I'll relate as much of the saga as I can before I fall asleep."

Dacy's jaw dropped, and the twins exchanged glances.

"We know you're really hurting if *you* need to crawl in bed in the middle of the day," Daria said.

"Come on." Dacy flanked her. "We'll get you to the room."

Daria took up a position on the other side. "We've got you, hon."

Cassidy stifled a laugh as they headed toward the elevator. If she passed out, she'd squish them both. She'd always felt like a giraffe compared with a set of dainty, prancing ponies.

Giraffe. That's what the kids had dubbed her as early as grade school. Hadn't it been Tim Halstead who first came up with that nickname? The memory was hazy. One of the Halstead brothers, anyway. Another reason never to trust one, even if he exhibited a few signs of decency as an adult. In her vast and agonizing experience, the Halsteads were about two things—whitewashing their image and making money, regardless of whom they hurt or ripped off. Best she remember that sordid fact the next time she was confronted by Tim's mesmerizing green eyes.

"Oh, Ms. Ferris!" a tenor voice called.

Cassidy and her cousins turned and answered, "Yes" in unison.

A pudgy man of medium height dressed in a suit and tie hurried toward them. If a facial expression could convey the wringing of hands, this guy's pulled it off.

"*Cassidy* Ferris. We are grateful to see you back

among us." He halted before them, gaze fixed on Cassidy. "And not seriously injured, I take it?"

"Not as seriously as I might have been. And you are?"

"Forgive me." He tendered a slight, old-fashioned bow. "Jason Clement, the concierge at the Aspen Grand Lodge. We are committed to providing our guests with the finest in service. Such an…" He hesitated, gaze darting this way and that, as if on the lookout for eavesdroppers, which were in short supply at the height of a fine day for skiing. "Such an incident as the one you experienced has never occurred here before. Please be sure to let the staff know if there is anything we can do to make you more comfortable."

"Thank you for your concern. At the moment, all I want is a soft bed and a deep pillow."

"I shall instruct the staff that you are not to be disturbed until you let us know otherwise. Particularly if any of the reporters return looking for you." The concierge's thin lips twisted.

Reporters? Of course there would be interest from the news services about a murder attempt on the ski slopes. No wonder Concierge Clement was hyper.

She kept the observation to herself and merely nodded. "I would appreciate that."

The elevator dinged, and Cassidy needed no urging to step into the car. The door closed on

Jason, who stared after them with anxious eyes. Something about the guy bugged her—other than his patent insincerity.

"Now that's what I call a bona fide cover-your-hiney attempt." Dacy snorted.

"Lame save-your-bacon move, that's for sure," Daria agreed. "Paul, the guy I'm going to supper with, says there's a rumor going around that our concierge is on thin ice with his employers, but they've cut him some slack time to get his medications regulated. I can see why he needs them." She narrowed her eyes at Cassidy. "You'd better not fall asleep before you let us in on the exact nature of this 'incident' that has Mr. Officious turning himself into a pretzel to avoid negative press."

As soon as they arrived at their shared room, Cassidy started her tale of the morning's events. She managed to change into a pair of cozy pajamas and swallow a pain pill before mentioning Tim. As she had suspected, the twin's horror that someone had taken a shot at their cousin was eclipsed by shock and fury that a Halstead dwelt under the same roof.

Daria threw up her hands. "Whatever happened out there, a Halstead is behind it."

"Make sure the cops get on his scent pronto." Dacy shook a finger at Cassidy as she slipped beneath the sheets of her queen-size bed.

The twins perched side by side on the edge of the one they shared.

"Maybe this time justice can be served." Daria crossed her arms.

"Lynching is too good for him." Dacy scowled.

Cassidy yawned and let her head sink into the down-filled pillow. "As preposterous as it sounds, Tim was quite helpful today. If I'd never met him before, I'd probably like him."

"Like him!" Dacy screeched.

"Francine would turn over in her grave," Daria growled.

They were still spewing dire threats and predictions as Cassidy faded into blessed slumber. She awoke to a quiet, vacant room dimmed by drawn blinds, though a hint of sunlight outlining them suggested that she might not be too late to call her partner in Seattle and get him started looking into things. Cautiously sitting up brought on no resurrection of her former headache.

She retrieved her phone, and the digital clock on the face informed her that she was within minutes of missing the shift change at 5:00 p.m. Pacific time. She tapped the speed-dial number for the West Precinct PD. The desk patched her straight through to Elliot.

"Detective Graves." He answered brusquely on the second ring. Catching a call this late in the day on a Friday, particularly the Friday of a holiday weekend, was never a cop's favorite thing.

"Hey, it's Cass."

"Cass!" The tone of voice did a one-eighty from hard business to mellow civility. "How's the skiing?"

She told him about the day's events, and the one-eighty reversed and took on an undercurrent of simmering lava.

"Whatever you need me to do, I'm on it," he rumbled.

"Check on my previous cases. See who's on the loose these days with a potential score to settle." The background hubbub of bullpen activity tugged at Cassidy. She should have stayed home instead of being lured—well, more like coerced by her cousins, aided and abetted by her own mother—on this waste of a vacation.

"I'm on it! What else?"

"I've run into an old enemy here, only he's acting like a long-lost friend. Tim Halstead. You know the family?"

"As in Halstead Enterprises? One of Thomas Halstead's boys?"

"The same." She would have been surprised if the name hadn't meant anything to him, though she'd never discussed with her partner her personal history with the family. The Seattle PD had its teeth on edge over the way the Halsteads eluded legal consequences. They were harder to pin down than moving shadows.

"If the Halsteads are involved, we're going to have to tread lightly," he said. "You know what I mean?"

Unfortunately, Cassidy did. Thomas Halstead, CEO of the company and Tim and Trace's father, was tight with vast numbers of city and state officials.

"I don't *know* that the Halsteads have anything to do with the attempts on my life. There's no way Tim took that shot at me, and he sure wasn't behind the wheel of that car."

"Could have hired someone."

"But why? To start with, I'd like to know what Tim's been up to since high school. Shouldn't be too hard to discover without creating ripples."

"I'll call you back as soon as I have something."

Cassidy set her phone down and got out of bed, still moving slowly lest she trigger a return of that killer headache. After a trip to the small but ornate bathroom and a refreshing face wash, she donned a pair of comfortable jeans and a sweatshirt then brushed her hair—taking gentle care around her wound. She'd discovered at least one advantage of possessing thick wire sprouting out of her head: it covered a bandage nicely.

Her ringtone sounded, and she jumped. *Get a grip, girl.* She gave herself a mental shake as she returned to the side table and grabbed the phone. All zeros in the caller ID slot, which meant a call from law enforcement. Elliot already?

"You were right," he announced without preamble. "It wasn't hard to check on Tim Halstead. You are flat not going to believe where he's employed."

"Tell me."

At Elliot's reply, Cassidy's fingers lost their grip and the phone thumped to the carpet.

Tim looked up from his meal to find a meteor named Cassidy descending on him. Something had lit her up.

The main dining room was filled with laughing, chattering guests, discreetly infiltrated by uniformed waitstaff.

Dacy and Daria had left the lodge restaurant a short time ago in the company of a pair of guys he recognized as fellow guests. Thankfully, the twins hadn't noticed him. Where had Cassidy been? Worries about her had nibbled at the back of his consciousness all afternoon, but he'd seen no sign of her—until now.

She stopped in front of the table he was sharing with several other casually met guests. "Tim, may I speak with you?"

The polite wording of her question contrasted starkly with the electric charge in her gaze.

"Will I survive the encounter?" He laid his fork beside his all-but-clean plate.

"Depends on how you answer a few questions." The tiniest grin softened her expression. "I'm too hungry for real food to waste time chewing you up and spitting you out."

"In that case—" Tim rose "—let me buy you supper while I treat myself to a slice of that cheesecake on the dessert cart."

"No need to buy me anything, Tim, but yes, let's grab that little table in the corner."

Tim excused himself and followed Cassidy's panther stride toward the isolated table.

"I'm glad to see you with no pinch between your eyebrows and color in your face," he told her as they were seated.

"I'm glad to be minus the concussion headache."

"Improvement doesn't mean you shouldn't take care not to reinjure your head."

"We're on the same page, Dr. Halstead." Her dry tone was accompanied by a smile.

Warmth spread through his chest. "What, exactly, did you need to ask me?"

The arrival of a waiter halted Cassidy's response. They ordered and then made small talk until the beverages arrived. Was she as amazed as he was at how natural this situation felt—like a genuine couple?

When the waiter withdrew at last, Cassidy

leaned toward him. "I'm going to ask you some questions. Don't elaborate, just say yes or no. We can sort out the fine points later—depending on your responses."

A knot formed beneath Tim's breastbone. He was being examined like a witness on a stand. Should he refuse to play the role? Then again, she had more right than most to stick his feet to the fire.

Deliberately, he relaxed in his chair and took a sip of water. "Proceed, but I reserve the right to object on my own behalf."

"Fair enough."

"Your family runs the largest housing industry on the West Coast, with holdings in Seattle, San Francisco and Los Angeles."

"That was a statement, not a question."

"I'm getting there. Would it be a fair assessment to say that a large share of their business dealings could qualify them as slumlords?"

Tim's eyes widened, but he had no doubt of the answer. "Yes."

Cassidy stiffened. "You admit it?"

"I'm under no illusions about what my family does."

"Would you testify to it?"

"If I could."

"That wasn't a yes-or-no answer. Why can't you?"

"I have no more proof than the PD does that

Halstead Enterprises cuts corners in construction and buys their way out of code violations."

"But you know about it."

"In a hearsay sort of way. Not admissible in court."

"You're elaborating."

He shrugged. "I'm a lawyer."

"A lawyer who started at Harvard as an undergrad on Daddy's dime, but then you left the Ivy League before your second year and inched and eked your way to a law degree at less expensive universities. Correct?"

"Yes."

"And now—" she played a drumroll on the table with her fingers "—you serve the needy as a legal aid attorney, defending the indigent and homeless in San Francisco?"

"That would be me."

Cassidy sagged as if deflated. "Legal aid attorneys are not well paid. You've got to be struggling to make ends meet, just like any other regular Joe. How did you afford to come to this resort for the weekend?"

"No mystery there. A friend won a trip for two—some radio giveaway—and shared his free pass with me. He'd decided we unattached fellows should go in search of the women of our dreams. Then he bugged out when he found her right there in San Fran. I almost didn't come alone, but the opportunity for stellar skiing was not to be passed up." Tim took another sip of water. "I could ask you the same thing. A Seattle cop doesn't make enough to rub elbows with the pampered set."

The smiling waiter arrived with Cassidy's meal and Tim's dessert.

"If you must know, Tim—" Cassidy shook out her napkin and spread it in her lap "—my grandmother left me a small nest egg. I used the bulk of it for my education. When the twins—who come from tidy money—announced their intention of coming here for the New Year's weekend, my family ganged up on me to tap into my bequest and join Dacy and Daria for what my mother described as 'a much-needed vacation.' Frankly, I prefer work to this sort of socializing, but I'm a wimp where my family is concerned. However, as you are under no illusions about your family's nature, I'm not fooled by mine. The whole idea is about getting me married off. My mother is rabid for grandchildren, and I'm an only child. Enough of an explanation?"

Cassidy's cheek color had deepened to hot pink, and Tim chuckled. "I envy your problem. My family's usual modus operandi is significantly less well intended."

His smile faded as he took a bite of the cheesecake. No doubt the confection was as delicious as it looked, but for him it had become pretty tasteless.

"Why *did* you break away from your family?" Her eyes dissected him.

"You know," he said, returning her stare.

The air around them thickened, as if weighted with tears. A name hung between them: Francine.

Moisture glazed Cassidy's gaze. "I wish I could believe that."

"It's the truth. The proverbial last straw. The first straw was laid at prom. You know which one."

"Yes."

Cassidy cleared her throat, ducked her head and began shoveling food into her mouth. At the speed she ate, she couldn't be enjoying a single bite. Tim cleaned up the cheesecake, not enjoying his food either.

He cast around in his mind for a way to continue the conversation, but found no words. What he wanted to say about that horrible prom was likely to implode what little credibility his career choice might have built with her. She was already chewing on too much new information along with her supper.

At last, she flung her napkin down beside her half-empty plate and stood up. "I'm going for some exercise. I have a lot to think about."

"I know," Tim said as he rose from his seat. "I get that you need a little space, but I'm not crazy about you wandering around alone."

"Believe me, I understand the need for caution.

I'll change into sweats and take the elliptical in the exercise room for a spin. I doubt I'll be alone in there. No need for you to get any sudden urges to use the treadmill."

Tim lifted his hands. "Far be it from me to intrude on a lady's thoughts."

"Then we understand each other."

He cocked his head. "Not yet. But we've made a start."

Cassidy scowled. "Don't push it. I respect you for turning over a new leaf, but you're still a Halstead. My humiliation at the prom is a small thing. It can be forgotten. But nothing can bring Francine back. Her loss is a permanent hole in our family."

She turned and walked away. Heart a sodden lump in his chest, Tim watched her go.

Despite her words, she hadn't forgotten the prom incident…or forgiven. And even if she did, she'd never be able to see past his identity as a member of the family responsible for Francine's senseless death.

The official determination of the cause of the apartment building blaze was a short in the basement electrical box. The electrician had been prosecuted—unsuccessfully—and as usual, Dad's company had skated away unscathed. Tim could understand how galling that circumstance must feel to the Ferris family.

How could he expect them to understand that

his position was, in some ways, worse? He had to live every day with the suspicion that something more sinister than negligence brought about the fire that razed a worthless building and cost a priceless life.

FOUR

Five minutes on the elliptical machine? That's all she could do? Cassidy rubbed her throbbing head. Clearly, her brain was not ready to handle the blood pumping through it at an elevated rate. Humiliated, she slunk out of the exercise room under the speculative gaze of several sweating patrons. Helplessness might be her top dreaded situation, but weakness came in a close second.

God, are You trying to teach me something?

Since Francine's death in one of Halstead Enterprises' firetraps, and the utter lack of justice following, she and the Lord had been on distant terms. Her fault, not His, but she didn't know how to fix the situation. Her trust in Him had taken a serious hit, and her faith had been hemorrhaging ever since.

"Ms. Ferris!" a stranger's voice called from the intersection of the hall that led to the exercise room and the one that went toward the pool and spa area.

Cassidy whirled, her fingers automatically searching for the weapon in a shoulder holster that wasn't there. A hulking man with stooped shoulders and salt-and-pepper hair took a step backward. One hand gripped a small notebook and a pen. Journalist. Not the most welcome sight, but not the least either. Tension drained from Cassidy's spine, and her hand dropped to her side.

"Nick Berglun with the *Aspen Times*. May I ask you a few questions about the attempts on your life?"

"You can ask, but I'll answer with 'no comment.' I prefer not to say anything that might compromise the police investigation."

"I understand you're an officer yourself." The aging giant drew closer, gray gaze sifting her.

Cassidy restrained herself from retreating. She wasn't used to feeling dwarfed. "A detective with the Seattle PD. No jurisdiction here. Just a regular citizen."

"Cass, this local yokel bothering you?" Stew strode up to them.

He was still wearing his sheriff's department uniform, though he must be off duty by now. Stew gazed up at the reporter, Nick stared back, and they grinned at each other. Friendly banter between a local newshound and an area law dog. Cassidy joined the smiles, but a movement behind the newsman and the deputy caught her eye, and her grin faded.

Half a face had peeked around the corner of the intersecting hallways and then abruptly pulled back, but not fast enough to prevent recognition. That jumpy concierge. Someone must have tipped him off that a reporter was in the building, but that didn't allow him a free pass to spy on her. She'd have a talk with him later.

"Any update you can give the press, Deputy?" Nick asked.

"Whatever the sheriff has told you is the extent of what we're ready to release."

"Not enough crumbs to feed a bird, much less the hungry public." The reporter chuckled.

"Here's something you can put in print," Cassidy said. "I plan to cut my vacation short and return to Seattle tomorrow. If someone's after me, they can take it up with me on my home turf. Your hungry public should be relieved to have me draw the threat of violence away from their area."

Nick scribbled in his notebook. "Peace and safety doesn't make hot copy, but I'll take cool news any day over tragedy. Good luck to you, Ms. Ferris." He saluted her with a tap of his pen to his forehead and strode away.

Stew reached into his belt and pulled out a small pistol. "Here's an extra piece on loan from the department. Drop it off tomorrow on your way out of town."

"Thanks." Her fingers closed around the cold, hard butt of the gun. She checked the load and found the chamber full, safety on. "Good to go." She tucked the weapon into the waistband of her sweatpants, near the pocket that contained her cell phone, and covered the butt with her T-shirt. "Your people find a bullet in that aspen tree?"

"Negative, but there's a small branch broken off about head height. If a bullet did that, it's buried in a snowdrift somewhere, and we'll never find it."

"Head height? That's weird. I was on the ground under the tree. No branches within feet of me."

The deputy shrugged. "The break was fresh, but could've been done by the wicked wind we had last night. Weather's been unpredictable as all get out this season, taking a toll on the quality of the snow and ice for recreation. First freezing, then thawing…and wind!" He let out a low whistle. "Tourism's been down because of it."

Cassidy huffed. "That explains why lodge staff would be nervous about bad publicity. Could the point of all this be to scare me, rather than kill me?"

"We can't assume that."

"If only we had a handle on motive."

"When we figure that out, we'll likely have the perp, too."

"My partner is looking into the past-case angle."

"It's the possibility that makes sense right now. Get some rest, Cass."

"You, too."

"Take care." Stew lifted a hand and sauntered toward the lobby.

Cassidy headed for the elevator. If she ran into that concierge on the way, he'd better watch out. She was cranky as a prodded badger. A few strides from the elevator button, the door dinged open, and Dacy and Daria spilled out, dressed in bright, flowing skirts, hair done up in casual elegance and makeup perfectly understated. Only one thing was missing—their dates.

"There you are!" cried one.

"You scared us out of our minds!" said the other.

Cassidy halted. "What do you mean?"

"We went up to check on you, and you weren't in our room." Daria spread her manicured hands.

Cassidy crossed her arms. "I appreciate you two looking out after me, but you know I can take care of myself."

"We know *you* think you can," Dacy said. "And most of the time *we* think you can, but this is, like, way crazy circumstances."

"Agreed, but after tomorrow morning, you won't have me on your plate. I'm going back to Seattle, where I have access to the resources to help me figure out what's going on."

"We're coming, too," said Daria. "Double sets of eyes to watch your back."

"Not happening. Your mother would shoot me for putting you in the line of fire."

"You know that's not true," Dacy said softly.

"She'll have our hides if we don't do all in our power to protect you." Daria lifted her chin.

Twin pairs of determined eyes set in dainty faces turned Cassidy's insides to mush. She wrapped her arms around the slender shoulders of her cousins.

"However did I get so blessed to be born into this family?" She set them away from her. "Here's the deal. I'm going up to our room to stay put. You two enjoy your evening. I think your guys are waiting." She waved a hand toward a pair of good-looking men in sweaters and chinos eyeing them from the vicinity of a massive wooden pillar. "In the morning, you can see me off on the plane. I'll have Elliot meet me at the other end. Easy peasy. I can get on about what I need to do, and you two won't have to miss the Countdown to Midnight banquet you've been talking about for weeks. Go on, now. Shoo!"

The duo drifted in the direction of their dates.

Daria turned and wagged a finger at her. "This discussion isn't finished yet."

Dacy swept an artfully stray curl from her face.

"Fasten the dead bolt, will you? We'll knock to be let in, and we won't be out late."

She waved them away, but lingered, watching the tender byplay of budding interest between newly met couples. The smiles. The laughter. The bright gestures.

Cassidy never felt that comfortable in the presence of romantic interest. The giraffe in her came out in social situations. She'd never be a girlie-girl like the twins…or the mischievous flirt Francine had been. Not that Cassidy had wanted to become the latter, but Frani had possessed a vulnerability about her that made a person excuse a lot of high-spirited nonsense. For the most part, Cassidy had made peace with life as the eternal tomboy. Lots of women were athletic and not particularly dainty—just not any of the women in her family.

Suppressing a sigh, she punched the button on the elevator.

"Mind if I ride up with you?" Tim's voice sent a pleasant shiver up her spine.

She'd been so wrapped up in her maudlin thoughts she hadn't heard his approach. Instead of Tim, the killer could have been the one who successfully sneaked up on her.

Frowning, she turned toward him. "It's a free elevator."

"Don't mind if I do then."

The door opened and they stepped in side by side.

"What floor?" she asked.

"Third."

"Same as mine." But there were only three, so being assigned to the same floor wasn't that strange.

They exited the elevator, and Cassidy allowed Tim to precede her up the hallway. What do you know? They were in the same wing.

"No way!" she cried out as Tim stopped in front of a door, keycard ready.

"What?" He squinted at her.

"You're in the room next to us."

His eyes widened. "This is creepy, Cass. I mean, not that I mind having the adjacent room, but there are too many coincidences. It's like we're being thrown together for some devious purpose."

Cassidy's stomach clenched. "Whoever took a shot at me this morning—did he intend for you to find my dead body? Then, when that attempt failed, did the killer plan for you to watch me get run over?"

A muscle in Tim's jaw flexed. "In a twisted sort of way, I may be as much of a target as you are."

"In that case, we're barking up the wrong tree looking for motive in my occupation."

Tim nodded. "We're going to have to talk about our shared history."

Cassidy's stomach clenched. Breaking open

those scars would likely reveal deep wounds that were as fresh as ever.

Tim shifted from one foot to the other, gaze traveling over the trappings of female occupancy—makeup, jewelry and perfume on the dresser, spike-heeled shoes tipped on their sides on the carpet. How many of these things were Cassidy's? He'd wager not many. Not that she needed to fuss over her appearance. He liked the natural way she presented herself—liked it too much for his own good.

"I'm not sure which is more risky," he said, "having your cousins catch me in your room, or inviting you into mine and having them freak out because you're not where you're supposed to be."

Cassidy chuckled. "I prefer our chat take place on my turf, so I'll take the blame. Don't sweat it, Halstead."

"Halstead. That's my point." He gingerly sat on the edge of a chair as she settled into one across from him.

Tim cleared his throat. "Let me start out by saying something I didn't have the guts or the decency to say at the prom that night."

Cassidy's stare froze on his face. Deer in the headlights didn't do her expression justice.

He leaned toward her. "I am heartily sorry for that whole debacle."

"Debacle?" She released a thread of a laugh. "You picked up an ivory tower vocabulary in law school." She shook her head. "Scratch that. As you may have noticed, I use sarcasm as a shield against pain."

Tim offered a slight smile. "Does it work?"

"Not so well."

At least she was trying to remain honest and open.

"I didn't mean to push you," he said.

She went stiff as a stick. "What are you talking about? You shoved me in the back. Hard! I hit the fancy spread on the punch table full-length and face-first. The entire table collapsed. Food flew everywhere. Punch sprayed like a geyser onto everyone within ten feet. And there I was, sprawled in the middle of the mess, all eyes focused on the clumsy giraffe."

Color blazed from Cassidy's face like a neon stoplight, but it was too late for Tim to halt.

"You're *not* a clumsy giraffe."

"That's a funny statement coming from the guy who gave me the nickname."

"It wasn't me!"

"Maybe it was Trace then."

"I have no recollection where that stupidity got started. Besides, the goofy misnomer didn't stick long. You beat up anyone who called you that. Trace even came home with a fat lip one day." Tim chuckled. "I always did wonder why I never had the pleasure of becoming acquainted with your wicked right hook."

The corners of Cassidy's lips tilted upward. "It's not too late to find out, Halstead."

"I'll pass." He waved a hand. "The name must have lodged in your head longer than anyone thought."

"All my life. At home, I have a giraffe collection. My way of thumbing my nose at the sting."

Tim's heart let out a long sigh. How the careless cruelties of youth dogged a person. "You're a gutsy woman, Cassidy Ferris. I've always thought that, but you're also human and vulnerable. There's no need to pretend otherwise."

"Oh, but I do need to. Thanks, anyway, for noticing my feelings. Too bad you didn't think about that when you decided it might be fun to give me that shove." Her gaze went flat.

"I didn't *decide* to embarrass you. Believe it or not, I was humiliated, too, but I hid my feelings under a show of bravado. Somebody tripped me, and you unwittingly broke my fall."

Her eyes narrowed. "You were tripped? By whom?"

"I'd give my last nickel to know. The place was hopping. I was heading for the table to get some refreshments for my date and me, something snagged my right ankle, I lurched forward into the person in front of me, and the rest of the story you know."

"Why didn't you explain back then?"

"With your buds baying for my blood? And my buds snickering and patting me on the back? I wasn't mature enough to set the record straight. Nor was I a Christian then."

Silence fell, except for a harsh rasp of strained breathing—hers and his.

"I'm trying to believe you, Tim." She wrapped her fingers together in her lap tightly enough to whiten her knuckles. "When did you come to faith in Christ?"

"Shortly after Francine died. I'd been working up to it, but that horror pushed me over the edge."

"At least something good came out of the loss of her life. I think she'd be pleased her tragedy reformed a Halstead."

"We don't all need reforming. I have praying grandparents, as well as aunts, uncles and cousins of integrity."

"No, I didn't know. How do they feel about the path your father has chosen?"

"About like you would expect. Believe it or not, my dad and Trace are the mavericks in our family herd."

Cassidy let out a soft whistle under her breath. "We attended the same schools all our lives. How come nobody knew these things?"

"Because Trace and I weren't acquainted with our extended family. On my dad's side, they hail from the East Coast. The only evidence we had of their existence were birthday cards and Christmas presents from faceless grandparents. On my mom's side, there are no close relatives. She was an only child, and her parents passed away before she married Dad. Then she died when Trace was born and I was a little short of fourteen months old. For our entire childhood, all we had in the world was Dad and each other."

"Wow!" Cassidy's back melted against her chair, her amber gaze dark and fluid. "The old phrase 'I'm blown away' doesn't begin to cover this. Everybody knew you and Trace were motherless and basically raised by a series of nannies and housekeepers. Sometimes I would try to write off your more offensive behaviors to that deficient upbringing. But the rest of this? My brain is scrambling to pick up pieces of shattered beliefs and rearrange the entire picture."

Tim leaned forward, elbows on his knees, hands clasped. "You can imagine the upheaval in my world when I came to faith and reached out to extended family, only to find they'd been clinging to me in prayer for years."

"I'm not sure I can grasp the magnitude." She shook her head. "My whole life is so rooted in family going back generations in multiple directions that my cousins are more like siblings."

"Don't I know it!"

Cassidy offered a lopsided grin that sent Tim's heart into tailspins.

"That may be the understatement of the year," she said. "If you're now tight with your extended family, why haven't you moved closer to them?"

Tim scratched the top of his head. "I ask myself the same question fairly often. Sometimes I think I'm compelled by an overactive guilt mechanism. Working for legal aid on the West Coast affords my only opportunity to head off or reverse some of the travesties Halstead Enterprises regularly commits."

"Travesties." Cassidy laughed. "Another la-de-da word, but it's appropriate. I'm surprised you're allowed to handle cases involving close family members. Doesn't that constitute some sort of conflict of interest?"

"It does." He nodded. "I don't litigate those cases. Legal aid attorneys up and down the coast come around to pick my brain about what makes Thomas and Trace Halstead tick—how they think. We've succeeded in landing a few wallops on the company lately, not merely the usual slaps on the hand."

Cassidy surged from her chair and paced across the room. "Tim, this is like dynamite exploding all kinds of assumptions set in stone. I can see how your father and brother could have a vendetta against *you*. How that might involve trying to kill *me*, I'm not sure I see a connection."

"I fervently hope we're hunting on the wrong scent," Tim said, "but out on that ski slope this morning, you told me you'd recently had a run-in with Trace. What was it about?"

She stopped pacing and shrugged. "A chance encounter at the courthouse where I'd just finished testifying, and Trace was strutting out of another courtroom in his designer suit and alligator boots. He sneered in my direction, and I'm afraid I responded with a snide remark about the city needing to install a revolving door on the courthouse strictly for Halstead use."

Tim winced. "Yikes! I can imagine how fast that statement got under Trace's thin skin."

"Not so much…which surprised me, but I think he was distracted by a known drug dealer that strolled past us and nodded to him like he was an old friend. Trace ignored him—and me—like the bedbugs his company denies their buildings have, and walked off without a word. The uncharacteristic self-control made me suspicious."

"What are you getting at?" Tim crossed his arms.

"I don't think Trace is satisfied with the income generated through the housing business. He's all about fast women, faster cars and the fattest wallet." She leaned toward him. "I suspect your brother has expanded operations into the kinds of things that go on after dark in those tenements of theirs."

"Like?"

"Prostitution...drugs—"

"Now, wait one red-hot second." Tim reared back, heat roasting his veins. "My dad may have rotten ethics when it comes to profiting from the poor. Even has some twisted self-justification about providing them with housing 'appropriate to their economic status.' But he's a fire-breather against human trafficking and drug dealing."

"I didn't say your dad's in the loop."

Tim froze and met Cassidy's stare. "Have you got any proof?"

"I've been conducting an extremely covert investigation and bits and pieces are starting to come together. Like I said, nothing to take to the district attorney yet, but I believe I'll get there."

"Does Trace know you're on his scent?"

"I hope not yet."

"But you don't *know* he's unaware."

She shook her head.

"If my brother is behind the attempts on your life and sucking me into them for some arcane purpose, how did he get us both here at the same time? I thought you said the trip was Dacy and Daria's idea."

"And my mom's." Cassidy rolled her eyes. "I took ribbing for weeks from my squad members as soon as they found out I was going to Aspen for a swanky weekend of romance. Remarks about placing Prince Charming under arrest and hauling him back to Seattle. Lame stuff like that. Surely you know Halstead Enterprises has informants on the force. They could have shared my plans with him. Once your brother knew where I was going to be, the only trick was luring you here at the same time."

"Are you serious?" Tim cocked his head. "Trace arranged some bogus radio giveaway and rigged it so that a friend of mine would win and just happen to give the prize to me? That's a tall stretch."

"No stretch at all if Trace was able to bribe or blackmail your friend into passing along the so-called prize from a contest that never happened."

Tim pawed his cell phone from his belt. "I'm calling Brad to ask right now."

"Put the phone away, gumshoe. Let's do our homework first."

"As in?"

"The lodge marketing director will know if the Aspen Grand held such a contest. If she denies it, then you've got a big crowbar to use in prying the truth from this supposed friend."

"We'll have to wait until morning then. I'm sure she's gone home for the day."

Cassidy pursed her lips. "A manager may be present who could answer the question tonight."

"Who?"

"Our friendly neighborhood concierge. He was here an hour ago. I saw the sneak lurking around."

"Sneak?"

"He's afraid of negative press, and a journalist had caught up with me. Jason Clement was trying to lurk out of sight, but I spotted him."

"Let's go then."

A couple of minutes later they approached the concierge's office on the first floor. Light spilled into the hallway from the open door, along with muted jazz music.

"What do you know?" Tim jingled the change in his jeans pocket. "Hopefully, we're about to get answers. He's—"

A sharp crack sliced off the end of his sentence. He froze, staring at Cassidy, who went into a cop crouch and reached for something under her shirt.

"Get down and stay back," she barked. "That was a gunshot."

FIVE

Pulse throbbing in her throat, Cassidy edged along the wall. No further sounds, other than the music, emerged from the office. Tim's hot breath fanned the back of her neck. So much for minding her instructions. Typical Halstead.

"I'm going in," she murmured. "Don't follow until I say it's clear."

"Would a distraction help?" he whispered.

"What do you have in mind?"

Tim straightened, pulled a coin from his pocket and chucked it through the doorway. A sharp clink sounded deep inside the room. If a gunman awaited them, the noise would draw his attention, if only for a split second.

Cassidy leaped through the doorway, gun brandished. A faint cordite odor tinged the air. Her gaze fell on Jason Clement sprawled in the chair behind the desk. A red substance drooled from the left side of his lolling head. Blood. His arms dangled from limp shoulders, hands hidden behind the desk.

The killer might be crouched back there, waiting to pop her. She edged around the side of the desk then lowered her gun. Nobody lay in ambush, but a small pistol rested on the carpet near the fingertips of Jason's left hand. Considering his mental health issues, were they dealing with suicide? Or was it murder? If the latter, how did the perp escape the room without being seen?

Her gaze fastened on a door in the side wall. A restroom or did it lead to the next-door office, where the perp could have slipped out into the hallway? She stepped toward the mystery door.

"You okay, Cass?"

Tim's voice halted her, though she kept her eyes on the doorknob. He called her Cass? He'd done that a number of times. She ought to correct him. Then again, she should ask herself why she didn't mind the familiarity, but this was not the time for self-examination.

"I'm okay," she called. "The office is clear, but don't come in unless you want to have nightmares."

"Too late."

She looked over her shoulder to find a grim-faced Tim staring at the body.

"Don't touch anything, but look around for a note. There might be one if this is a suicide."

"Will do."

Cassidy proceeded to the suspicious door, wrapped her hand in the end of her T-shirt and gripped the very edge of the knob. It didn't turn. No keyhole, so it had to have been locked from the other side. The observation could be significant. Or it might mean nothing. That's how investigations went.

"I found something," Tim said.

She joined him by a printer situated on a credenza a few feet from the desk. A lone sheet of paper lay in the exit tray, but the printing was facedown. Her fingers itched to snatch the paper, but she curled them against her palms. She couldn't afford to take a chance of marring evidence with her prints.

"Would this help?" Tim held a pen out to her. "Came from my pocket, not anywhere in this room."

"In that case, thanks." She took the offering. "Don't mind if I do."

With the end of the pen, Cassidy lifted the sheet so that several lines of all-caps printing showed.

I WANTED SWEET REVENGE FOR US. I TRIED. TWICE. I DON'T HAVE THE COURAGE TO GO ON. NO JOB EITHER. I'M SURE TO BE FIRED SOON. I CAN'T HANDLE OUR FAMILY'S DISAPPOINTMENT IN ME. BEV, I'M SO SORRY.

No indication of the author—typed or otherwise. "Who's Bev?"

Tim asked the question that bugged Cassidy. The answer niggled in the back of her mind, but her memory wasn't one hundred percent on the idea, and it might be a long shot.

"I may be misinterpreting," Tim went on, "but could the concierge be the person who attempted twice to murder you? But revenge for what?"

"You're asking the right questions." Cassidy nodded. "The answer may lie in Bev's identity. If you would notify the front desk that there's been a tragedy, they'll call the local authorities. I need to call my partner at his home and have him check into something."

As she punched in Elliot's number, she sensed rather than saw Tim withdraw.

"Any developments, Cass?" Her partner came on almost right away.

"You could say that." She quickly filled him in. "I have a hazy recollection of participating in a bust that sent a couple of popular college students to the slammer for dealing drugs. I think the first name of one of them was Beverly, though her last name wasn't Clement. Would you do whatever you can to find out if this Beverly had some connection to the dead concierge? Old flame? Whatever?"

"Consider it done. I hope we find that connection. Then we can mop our brows, and you can enjoy the rest of your New Year's weekend."

"Har-de-har, partner. You know I never wanted to participate in this shindig."

Elliot laughed. "Go with the flow, Cass."

"Thanks. I think." She keyed off her phone.

If Jason Clement's note about double failure referred to the attempts on her life, and if her hunch panned out with Elliot, they would have established motive for Jason's murderous intentions toward her. His pre-existing mental instability made him ripe for suicidal despair. Such pat answers left the elements of coincidence that had thrown Tim and her together in this unlikely place unexplained. She didn't like loose ends, though in police work she sometimes had to accept them.

Could there be a deeper reason why Jason had to die? Was someone else involved? With the murder attempts apparently solved by the suspect's death, she might reasonably be expected to let her guard down, creating opportunity for…what? Another attempt on her life that might succeed?

Where did Tim fit into the picture? Was he a target, also? Or did he have something to do with causing the nasty events? Something deep inside rebelled against a "yes" answer to that last question. He certainly hadn't done in the concierge… unless he was the mastermind behind the original attempts. But that theory, coupled with the possibility that this was murder, not suicide, would necessitate a third accomplice, which seemed a clumsy and convoluted scheme for such a smart man. Besides which, why would Tim be after her?

Unless he was trying to protect Trace. He could have been lying about his estrangement from his family. No! She shook her head. What Elliot had told her about Tim and what Tim had told her about himself dovetailed and rang true.

As a cop, Cassidy's lie-o-meter had grown pretty sensitive. She'd seen the sincerity in his gaze when he told her about becoming a Christian and finding his extended family, as well as the pain that thinned his lips when he spoke of his rejection by his father and brother.

Of course, her lifelong unwelcome attraction to Tim Halstead could be clouding her judgment. There! She'd admitted the truth to herself. She had a thing for an old enemy, which in a sense made her a traitor to herself, not to mention Francine and the rest of her family. Could her illicit attraction also get her killed?

Was the danger finally over?

Tim leaned against a wall in the hallway outside the dead concierge's office just beyond the police crime scene tape.

Police and coroner staff buzzed in and out. Cassidy was in the thick of the swarm, but considerate enough to pause now and then to deliver updates. Probably not a courtesy the run-of-the-mill witness received from the cops.

Already, it had been established from interviews with shocked staff that Jason had been "acting funny" lately. Well, funnier than usual. Apparently, the guy was an odd duck altogether. Tim wasn't surprised. From what little he'd observed of the concierge on check-in and other brief sightings, he'd seemed highly nervous and more than a tad obsessive.

It had also been discovered that the door inside Jason's office connected with the office of the environmental services director. Provided the door was unlocked at the time the shot was fired, it would have been possible for a killer to duck through there, lock the door from that side and escape into the hallway when the coast was clear. It was equally possible that nothing of the sort had happened.

"Tim!" Cassidy strode out of the office, grinning. "Elliot—my partner—just called back. It's likely the 'Bev' mentioned in the note was Beverly Hansel."

She ducked under the crime scene tape and stood before him. "Three years ago, I stumbled on evidence that she and her husband were involved in a major drug-distribution ring operating on college campuses up and down the coast.

I participated in the bust and testified at the trial. Her family was bitterly angry with me then, and I imagine they are more so now. Bev was killed last month in a prison fight. Jason was her brother. Hansel was Bev's married name."

Then the attempts on Cassidy's life were over. A light-headed thrill shot through Tim.

What was up with the depths of this elation? How much did he care for this woman? However much it was couldn't bode well for his heart. Maybe he should leave Aspen—pack up and go. Right now.

Whoa! The sudden flight instinct was another bad sign.

He planted his feet and smiled. "That's great news! Well, not so great for his poor family."

She looked down. "I remember how it feels to get tragic news about a loved one."

Tim laid a hand on Cassidy's shoulder. "Don't torture yourself. You didn't make the bad choices for Beverly or Jason."

Her head came up, gaze fierce. "Francine's choices were made *for* her. It's not her fault her family fell on hard times and had to move into a substandard building. My folks offered to let her family live with us until they got back on their feet, but her dad wouldn't consider it. Too embarrassed. Proud. Then the fire...so senseless!" She buried her face in her hands.

Tim wrapped his arms around Cassidy, and she melted into him.

"Shh," he murmured, breathing in the pleasant strawberry scent of her shampoo. "None of them were to blame. It was *my* family..." Further words choked in his throat.

His father's lack of ethics, the contractors who slyly cut corners for greater profits, and the license and inspection officials who took cash under the table—these were the culprits. Why did the legal system seem powerless to stop the greedy tactics? Would justice ever be served?

"You're not to blame, either, Tim." Cassidy's breath caressed his ear as her words fell like gentle rain on his soul.

Never had he thought he'd hear a Ferris say such a thing to a Halstead. She drew back, but only far enough to look into his face. Tim's gaze fastened on the graceful curve of her lips.

"Coming through," a male voice called.

As a gurney wheeled out of the office, Cassidy broke free of Tim's embrace, and he let his arms fall to his sides. The white sheet that covered the gurney barely masked the shape of a human body. Tim swallowed hard.

"I'm going to my room." Cassidy turned her back on Tim.

"We might as well go together."

"Sure." The word was terse.

If he could see her face, it probably glowed bright red. Him? He must be stark white. *Lord, help me!* He'd been thinking about Cassidy Ferris's lips. His blood roared in his ears. Now he knew what terror felt like. A blow to his shoulder jarred him, and he suddenly remembered to breathe.

"What was that for?" He rubbed his arm and scowled at Cassidy.

She scowled back, and the tightness in his chest eased. He knew how to handle this return to normalcy between them.

"I asked if you knew a different route to the third floor than through the lobby, but you just stared off into space."

"We can take the back stairs."

"Let's do it."

A few minutes later, they exited the landing, and their doors came into view. Just in time to catch Dacy and Daria emerging from one of them. *Oh, goody.* Tim curbed the impulse to head back down the stairs. Cassidy had begun to semi-accept him—especially since their earlier conversation made headway on clearing the air about the prom incident. The twins knew none of the things he'd shared with their cousin. By their body language they were loaded for bear.

"Where have you been?"

"Are you trying to drive us out of our minds?"

"What are you doing with *him*?"

The machine-gun questions spurted from one and then the other and back again.

"Hold your fire," Cassidy said. "I'm fine, and Tim is part of the reason."

"You've got to be kidding," Dacy said.

Daria flung up her hands. "I'm beginning to think we're in Wonderland, not Colorado."

Cassidy chuckled. "If the next thing out of your mouths is 'off with his head,' I'm going to go all Mad Hatter on you."

Tim failed to feel amused as he dug his key-card from his pocket and stopped at his door. A hot shower, a little mindless television and soon to bed suited him down to the ground. Maybe he'd leave in the morning. The idea of skiing had lost its luster, and tomorrow evening's Countdown to Midnight banquet held no interest for him.

"Hang on a second, Tim." Cassidy touched his arm.

The mild gesture rooted him in place more effectively than a pair of shackles.

"Dacy, Daria," she said, "I want you to meet Tim Halstead, a brother in Christ."

The twins' mouths flopped open. They blinked at him as if he'd suddenly appeared out of thin air.

"Y-you're a Christian?" Dacy managed.

"Since when?" Daria's eyes narrowed.

Tim opened his mouth, but Cassidy waved a forestalling hand. "I'll fill you in later. Right now, it's more important that we tell you we've discovered the person who was trying to kill me, and he's no longer a threat."

The twins' faces lit up as exclamations of thanksgiving softened their entire aura. Clearly, they hadn't been down in the lobby or other public areas when the news hit the grapevine about the death. They'd probably be less enthused, but no less grateful, when they heard the exact circumstances of the discovery.

"Does this mean we can stay for the rest of the weekend?" Dacy folded her fingers together in a semblance of prayer.

"*You* can. I don't know that I'm up for a party." Cassidy wrinkled her nose. "I've got a ton to do back—"

"Like fun you're running out on us." Daria drew herself up to her full five foot one.

"Not when we've spotted a perfect date for you." Dacy bounced on her toes.

"Our dates will set you up with him like that." Daria snapped her fingers.

The twins exchanged hundred-watt grins. Cassidy's face froze. Pure panic if Tim had ever seen it.

She whirled toward him and grabbed his hand. "I've found my own date, thank you very much. And he's standing right here."

Tim wouldn't have taken a million bucks to miss the looks on Dacy and Daria's faces. Now *that* was funny. He'd enjoy the moment more if he wasn't sure escorting Cassidy Ferris to the banquet was the dumbest and most dangerous thing he'd ever done—but no guts, no glory.

SIX

Now Cassidy understood the precise meaning of the phrase "in the hot seat." If the hotel room chair beneath her actually burst into flames, she'd hardly be surprised. Not with the lasers blazing at her from two pairs of blue-gray eyes. After Tim had wisely withdrawn into his room, she and her cousins had entered theirs. Dacy and Daria had barely been persuaded to settle on the edge of their bed to hear her explanation of the evening's events—particularly her horrifying decision to consort with the enemy.

"Look, I haven't forgotten that Tim and Trace have been thorns in our sides since grade school," she said, "but I've discovered a few things today that change the picture—at least where Tim is concerned."

The twins crossed their arms and silently dared her to persuade them. Mustering her courage on a long inhale, Cassidy forged ahead. She'd never been one to babble, but she must be doing so in this long monologue of bizarre events compressed into a single day, as well as equally strange conversations with the last person in the world she thought she would ever trust. But Tim had proved himself rock solid under the direst of conditions.

"Whoa! Whoa! Whoa!" Daria lifted a hand. "You're telling us that Tim Halstead is estranged from his family?"

"No," Cassidy said. "I'm telling you that he's found his extended family, and he's estranged from his immediate family—by mutual choice, I understand."

"Plus he's working for legal aid against said immediate family?" Dacy shook her head.

"Way weird." Daria let out a soft whistle.

Cassidy laughed. "Tell me about it! This whole day has been one big sack of strange."

Dacy's eyes narrowed. "So who was trying to do in our favorite cousin?"

Cassidy told them about Jason Clement.

"You were right!" Daria cried. "The culprit was someone connected to one of your past cases."

"It would seem so." Cassidy picked at a speck of lint on her sweatpants.

"I know that look," Dacy said.

"Something isn't adding up for you," her sister added.

Cassidy shrugged. "Jason's connection to me is clear, but he has no link to Tim—no reason even to know him, much less drag him into the equation." She spelled out the reason she and Tim were headed to see the concierge.

Daria pursed her lips. "I see the striking coincidences, but maybe your mutual presence at the Aspen Grand is a separate issue from the concierge trying to kill you. Maybe Tim set up this 'accidental' meeting between you."

"Why would Tim deliberately plant himself in the path of three Ferrises in one place?" Cassidy laughed. "Do you think he has a death wish? Besides which, how would he know we'd be here?"

"I don't think there's any 'we' involved," Dacy said. "It's you he's interested in."

"Always has been." Daria nodded.

Cassidy stiffened. "What are you talking about?"

Dacy and Daria rolled their eyes in the kind of unison that made twins eerie from time to time.

"He's always had a thing for you," Daria said.

Dacy grinned. "Even when he was putting toads in your locker in grade school."

"Or snatching the cookie off your tray at lunch in junior high." Daria giggled.

"Or hiding your biology book in high school." Dacy smirked.

"*Especially* when he was doing those things." Daria nodded. "Though shoving you into the punch table at the prom was extreme."

Dacy scowled. "Since he's making nice this weekend, has he bothered to apologize?"

"As a matter of fact, he did." Cassidy's words came out rather faint.

Her breath had been stolen by her cousins' assessment of the historic interplay between her and Tim Halstead. She'd more than returned his dirty tricks with some of her own—except for the prom mess—but apparently he'd been as much a victim then as she was. Did Dacy and Daria see something going on between Tim and her that she'd never acknowledged before? Had they been acting out their mutual attraction in the only way possible when family loyalty was at stake?

"I hope he groveled."

Daria's proclamation short-circuited Cassidy's lightbulb moment. She shook herself. Fine theory, but she wasn't buying into it. Not yet.

"He did better than that," she told her cousins. "He explained."

"There is no explanation." Daria.

"Or excuse." Dacy.

"He was tripped," Cassidy said.

Silence swept over the room. Daria opened her mouth then shut it. Dacy looked toward her sister and then away.

"To answer the obvious question," Cassidy said, "he doesn't know who tripped him."

Dacy's face went white and then washed red. "I might." Her voice emerged in a mouse squeak.

Daria fixed her sister with a wide gaze. "You know something I don't know?" She asked the question as if the possibility was inconceivable.

"Don't hold back now." Cassidy's pulse rate spiked and her head began to ache.

"I think..." Dacy paused and gnawed her lower lip. "Well, I suddenly realized...it could have been Francine."

Daria lunged up from the bed and glared down at her sister. "Do you know what you're saying?"

Dacy rose, hands on hips, and met her twin's glare. "I'm not saying she planned for Tim to fall into Cassidy and knock her into the table. I think Frani was horrified by the consequences of her careless action, and that's why she took off like a scalded cat whenever anyone mentioned the incident."

Every nerve ending jangling, Cassidy crossed the space between them in two strides and gripped her cousin's shoulders. "Look me in the eye and tell me why you believe Francine is the one who tripped Tim."

Dacy blinked up at her. "She told me...sort of."

With a moan, Daria flopped backward onto the bed. "I have officially fainted."

"What did she say?" Barely daring to breathe, Cassidy let her hands fall to her sides.

"Frani got pretty down when they lost their house and had to move into one of the Halstead properties."

"I remember."

Daria sat up. "We tried to lift her spirits, but she was stuck on lemons and not having any sugar."

"I was giving her a pep talk a couple of weeks before the fire," Dacy went on, "telling her they wouldn't be stuck in that dump forever. Besides, she was about to graduate and move on with her own life. She gives me the strangest look—like something had scooped out her insides and left her hollow. Then she said, 'Dreams are fine for you, but I sold my soul the day I stuck out my big foot and made an enemy fall.' I've thought often about those words, but never made sense of the remark. Until now."

"How would doing what came naturally between Halsteads and Ferrises amount to selling her soul?" Cassidy gripped the sides of her throbbing head. "Why didn't she tell us?"

"After she saw how devastating the incident was for you?"

"Yeah," Daria agreed. "You know how sensitive she was. She couldn't risk alienating her cousin-sisters when her immediate family was on the skids."

"I'll bet guilt ate her alive." Dacy nodded.

Cassidy's legs turned to gelatin. She sank into a

chair. How different truth often was from perception. Yet how perfectly this scenario fit the facts. Hadn't she wondered during their senior year why Francine spent less and less time in her company? What a dunce she was for lumping all of Frani's mulligrubs into the basket of her family's financial woes, never noticing there might have been something more going on—something personal between the two of them.

Later that night, sleep eluded Cassidy. It didn't seem to be eluding the twins, though. For a couple of delicate dahlias, they snored and snuffled up a storm.

Grabbing her phone from the side table, Cassidy slipped from beneath the sheets and padded into the bathroom. She called the lodge front desk and asked for the call to be transferred to Tim's room number.

"Hello?" His voice was groggy, though he'd picked up after the second ring.

"It's Cassidy. I'm sorry for waking you."

"Did you change your mind about letting me escort you to the banquet?" His tone sharpened.

Did she dare believe she detected a note of disappointment?

"No such luck, Halstead."

He chuckled. Definitely a note of relief. Cassidy's spirits lifted. She hadn't totally shanghaied him after all.

"I'm not calling about the banquet," she said. "I thought you might like to know who tripped you at prom."

Several beats of silence pulsed through the connection. "One of the twins?" His words were tentative, as if tiptoeing through a tangle of live wires.

"Guess again. Who is no longer among us?"

"Wo-o-o-ow!" The exclamation was long and low and weighted with feeling.

"Dacy knew something she didn't know she knew, and we figured it out."

"I'm so sorry. You must feel terrible."

Cassidy's jaw tensed. "Why would *I* feel terrible? For accusing you of pushing me? It *was* the logical conclusion."

"That's not what I meant, Cass. I was talking about the two of you being robbed of the opportunity to make things right between you. I mean the whole sweet-confession-and-forgiveness thing."

Every raised hackle in her heart stood down. "You're a good man, Tim. I mean that. You officially have permission to call me Cass."

A low chuckle caressed her ear. "That's a relief, the way I keep risking your right hook with the liberties that slip out."

"See you tomorrow. Pick me up at five?"

"This may sound weird, but I'm looking forward to it."

"It's weird, all right, but nice."

Cassidy broke the connection. The smooth warmth coating her middle must be the effects of that forgiveness thing flowing between them. A better-than-good feeling. She wasn't about to make the mistake of reading anything more into it, though.

Nor was she finished looking into the "coincidences" that brought them here at the same time. An unseen hand operated behind the scenes. Of that she was sure. Was the purpose benevolent or quite the opposite?

After Cassidy called, Tim lay awake, staring at the shadowed ceiling. Closure on the tripping incident was a good thing, right? Then why did he remain uneasy?

Evidently, Francine never outright admitted her part in the incident. He could understand the reluctance to "fess up." But he couldn't understand why she suddenly started hanging out with Trace on the sly. Several times that summer between his graduation and heading off for college, he thought he'd glimpsed Francine riding in the passenger seat of his brother's car. When Tim asked, Trace denied it, and Tim had been too absorbed in his own life to pursue the matter. Maybe he should have.

In the morning, Tim stared into the mirror as he shaved, and questions about ancient history faded. More immediate questions surfaced. Such as should he tackle the slopes again or be a gentle-man and see if Cassidy wanted to go into Aspen with him and browse the shops, since she was restricted from more physical activities? The latter idea probably wouldn't fly. Unlikely that she was the kind to shop all day. That would be more the twins' speed.

Besides, he scowled at himself, and his image scowled back, whom was he fooling that his desire to hang out with her had anything to do with gentlemanly consideration? He just wanted to see her and could hardly wait for tonight.

"You're pathetic, Halstead," he told himself out loud then slowly lowered his razor.

Halstead. That was still his last name, and hers was Ferris. How did the family feud start anyway? The answer was lost in the mists of kindergarten.

Squaring his shoulders, he resumed shaving. The slopes it was then.

An hour later, he pushed off and started down the advanced slope. The temperatures today were considerably milder than yesterday, and the run was a bit sticky, slowing his descent.

Many skiers dotted the slopes. Not like yesterday near dawn when Cassidy and he had the area nearly to themselves. Then that fateful lone aspen tree hove into view. He went perpendicular and swished to a stop on the verge of the snowdrift that had offered Cassidy and him meager cover from a gunman. The impressions from where they crouched were visible in the packed powder, as was a streak of pink, marking the spot where she lay and bled.

Volcanic heat erupted in his gut. If the shooter wasn't already dead, he'd happily volunteer to throttle him. He examined the aspen tree. Scuffed bark and scrapes in the snow at the base of the trunk revealed where Cassidy had crashed. His gaze traveled up the trunk and stopped on a spot level with his head.

A small branch had been ripped off the tree straight in front of him. The branch wasn't lying on the ground, so the cops must have collected it as evidence. Had another bullet done that damage? If so—a chill speared through his marrow— then the sniper hadn't been aiming at Cassidy, but at him standing above her. By pushing him over the edge of the snowdrift, Cassidy probably saved his life.

But if the concierge was gunning for the cop who sent his sister to prison, why take a shot at a bystander? To eliminate a potential witness, or had Tim been lured here to become a part of the intended tragedy? He shook his head. The latter made less sense than the former, and yet the mystery of his presence at the same event as Cassidy, hundreds of miles from their respective homes, had not been solved.

Tim shoved off and finished the run then turned in his skis and headed up the trail on foot toward the lodge. Overhead, dark clouds twisted and gathered. The dampness in the air clotted in his lungs. Storm on the way?

He pulled his cell phone from his pocket and called Brad. He answered after the third ring.

"Hey, buddy, having a great time?" Brad's excessive joviality grated on Tim.

"Edge-of-your-seat exciting is more like it," he said.

"The slopes are that good? Lucky dog!"

"Wishing you'd ditched Bridget and come along?"

"Who?" A tick of silence stumbled past. "Oh, Bridget, yeah."

"There is no Bridget, is there, Brad? No free trip won through a radio contest either."

A thin chuckle stuttered in Tim's ear. "I told him you were too smart not to figure it out."

"Told who?"

"I know you aren't close with your family, but your dad wanted to give you a belated Christmas present without you knowing who it came from."

"My dad approached you to pull off this crazy stunt to send me on a holiday vacation?"

"Not in person, no. His office manager called me and set it up. Some guy named Glen."

Glen was his dad's office manager, all right.

But giving his rebel son a secret present out of the goodness of his paternal heart? Way too far out of character for credibility.

"You're a pal, Brad. Thanks for leveling with me."

"No problem. Too bad I'm not on your father's gift list."

You don't know how lucky you are, buddy. Tim keyed the phone off.

The path took him to the lodge's vast rear courtyard, wrapped in a U shape by the main building and wings on each side. A covered veranda looked out on the open area on all three sides. Small groups of guests occupied furniture clusters on the veranda. The damp atmosphere muffled the laughter and chatter. Other people, mostly couples, strolled along the cleared paths admiring ice sculptures displayed in the open courtyard. A lone figure drew Tim's attention.

Cassidy. Standing by the sculpture of a snowboarder near one corner of the courtyard, she had her back to him, phone to her ear. Tim lengthened his stride. She'd want to know what he had found out.

A sharp crack split the air, and the sculpture's head began rolling off its icy shoulders toward Cassidy. With a shout, Tim's football instincts propelled him into a charging tackle.

SEVEN

A sudden crack sent Cassidy into a crouch. Then a force hit her from behind and flung her toward a snowdrift. At the last instant, whoever had her in his grip flipped them over, and her attacker landed first with her on top, faceup. Her assailant's grunt competed in her ears with a shattering crash. Tiny ice shards geysered over them as she wrenched free and bounded to her feet in full self-defense posture.

Tim's wide, green gaze met hers. He sprawled in the snow, mouth agape, quite likely sucking for the breath that had been knocked out of him. Onlookers cried out and running feet converged on them, as she glanced back to find the ice-chunk head of the snowboarder turned to jagged splinters on the sidewalk. A shiver coursed through her that had nothing to do with the winter chill.

"Are you okay?" Cassidy reached a hand down to Tim, who accepted it and rose to his feet.

"Are *you* okay? That's the main thing."

"If you hadn't tackled me, I probably wouldn't be. That was close! Might not have killed me, but wouldn't have done my concussion any favors."

Excited guests crowded around, inquiring about their welfare. Then a slender, dark-haired woman dressed in the lodge uniform of gray slacks, white blouse and gray business jacket shouldered through the gathering. Her name badge read Mindy Ulstein, Manager.

"Please accept our deepest apologies for this… occurrence." She turned toward the crowd. "We will have our maintenance technician give the sculpture park a thorough inspection. Ladies and gentlemen, please withdraw to other locations until the inspection is complete."

"So you think other sculptures might be unsafe?" a woman inquired shrilly.

"I didn't say that, ma'am, though we would be lacking due diligence if we didn't inspect the sculptures after a piece has fallen off one. The unusual temperature swings this winter haven't done the quality of the ice any favors."

"There are too many dangerous things going on around here," the same shrill voice cried. The woman gazed up at a pinch-mouthed man who might be her husband. "Maybe we should leave."

Mindy's middle-aged face washed white. "I'm afraid no one is leaving today, or perhaps tomorrow either." She spread her hands in a placating gesture. "An ice storm has already closed in over the city of Aspen, and all planes are grounded. The storm will be here shortly, so indoor activities are advised for the remainder of the day. But that's not such a bad thing." The manager delivered a broad smile. "This evening's Countdown to Midnight banquet is not to be missed. You may wish to begin pampering yourself in the spa or beauty shop in preparation for the event."

Murmuring in conversation, guests began drifting toward the lodge entrances. Cassidy and Tim were left with the manager.

She turned toward them with an apologetic grimace. "You haven't had the most pleasurable visit with us, Miss Ferris. Your meals and room charges will be on the house by way of compensation." With a nod, she hurried away toward the lodge.

Cassidy frowned at Tim. "Do you really think the sculpture fell apart by accident?"

They turned as one and scanned the eerie remnants of the decapitated ice snowboarder.

"I don't know what else to call it," he answered. "If it was sabotage prepared in advance, you couldn't have been the specific target. There's no way a saboteur could know you would stand by this particular sculpture."

"True." She scanned the banks of windows that looked out on the courtyard. "But someone in any number of the rooms that face this direction could have shot the sculpture in the neck to send the head tumbling. Or maybe they were gunning for me and hit the statue instead. Remember, we didn't hear a shot when Jason Clement targeted me."

"Us," Tim said. "I was out on the advanced slope this morning and stopped at a certain aspen tree. If a second shot clipped the branch on that tree, the shooter was probably aiming for my head and only missed because you knocked me off my feet."

Cassidy let out a low whistle. "Makes sense. But why would Jason have wanted to kill you, too?"

"Eliminate a witness?"

"Witness to what? You didn't see anything."

"He couldn't know that."

Cassidy rolled her shoulders. "I'm not satisfied with that explanation. There's something... off about this whole situation. I was just on the phone with the local sheriff's office. Stew says they've discovered that Jason Clement owns a car consistent with the type that tried to run me over in Aspen and that he is an accomplished marksman. However, no silenced rifle has yet been found among his belongings."

"Maybe he ditched it."

"Or maybe someone remains at large in possession of a weapon capable of dealing silent death."

Tim tugged on her arm. "I'm uneasy standing out here. We'd better head inside."

They went into the lodge as Tim told her about the conversation with his friend Brad.

Pausing in front of the elevator, Cassidy raised her brows. "You're telling me your *father* arranged this trip for you?"

"I can't bring myself to believe it, though I believe that's what Brad was told."

"Another mystery."

"I intend to dig out the truth, even if it means ambushing Dear Daddy with a surprise visit."

"You haven't had any interaction with him since he disowned you?"

They entered the elevator, which was blessedly vacant.

"I tried to contact him when I heard about his car accident in Rio de Janeiro a year ago," Tim said as the car rose. "To check on him. He's still my father, after all. But Glen, his personal assistant, said my father was fine—just a fender bender—and he didn't care to speak with me."

Cassidy's heart wrenched at the pain in those vivid green eyes.

"What do you say we lay our troubles aside and enjoy ourselves this evening?"

The shadows fled Tim's gaze. "I'll pick you up at five."

"I'll be ready." Cassidy stretched her lips into a smile.

Did her expression look even remotely natural? Yes, she was on edge about the possibility that Jason had an unidentified accomplice, but the threat of murder didn't hold a candle to the terror of tonight's formal event on the arm of Tim Halstead.

Endless hours later, Cassidy stood in front of a full-length mirror in the bathroom. Her cousins, also in formal attire, hovered on each side of her. All afternoon, they had prodded her from one primp session to the next. She'd joined them in receiving a facial, a manicure and a pedicure. Her hair had been professionally styled, and the twins had personally seen to her makeup and accessories—a silk orchid strategically placed in her upswept hairdo and sparkly bling dangling from her ears, neck and wrist. And then there was the gown she and her cousins had picked out during an all-day shopping ordeal right after Christmas.

Cassidy blinked at herself. Who was this woman in the mirror?

"Soooo elegant," Dacy cooed.

"Forget Halstead." Daria laughed. "The guys are going to be tripping over each other to introduce themselves."

Cassidy snorted. "I'm the one who trips. Remember?"

Dacy sniffed. "I think it's time to forget."

"Amen to that." Daria nodded. "It's been established that clumsiness was not a factor in the prom disaster, and I think it's time you believe that."

"So, what do you think, Cass?" Dacy posed the question, hands on hips. "Be honest."

Cassidy had to admit the full-length emerald gown with spaghetti straps looked as good on her as anything she'd ever worn. The color emphasized infinitesimal greenish flecks in her amber eyes and contrasted nicely with her black hair. The low waist and fitted cut of the hips and torso above a flared skirt made the most of her height— or, rather, the least of it. Her strappy sandals had no heels, and the gown's hem kept her flipper-size feet covered.

She actually felt presentable, maybe even pretty. A tiny smile began to grow on her carefully rouged lips.

"You are beautiful, Cass!"

Daria's proclamation sent a spark through Cassidy of…what? Hope? She glanced from one to the other of her beaming cousins. They really did love her, and she'd take their high regard over grace and beauty any day.

"I think I'm going to enjoy myself tonight," Cassidy said as she smoothed the gown over her lean middle.

"Awesome!" Dacy did a funky jig that set them to giggling as if they were back in grade school.

A knock sounded, and Cassidy froze. She glanced at the watch she'd laid on the bathroom vanity. Five on the dot. Her heart turned inside out. Tim was punctual. Now if only she could work up the courage to answer the door.

What look would she detect on his face when he beheld Cassidy Ferris in formal attire for the first time since high school?

Standing at Cassidy's door, waiting centuries for it to open, Tim ran a finger between his neck and the collar of his dress shirt. Funny, this tie had never strangled him before. Now he could scarcely breathe.

His skittery heart echoed the rattle of the latch as the door swung open by an unseen hand. Oxygen fled the atmosphere. A stunning woman stood framed by the doorway, perfect from the orchid gracing her ebony waves to the brightly painted toenails peeping from beneath the hem of her stellar gown.

Cassidy.

But not Cassidy.

At least not the Cassidy who'd pushed him down on the playground when they were in first grade for putting a spider in Dacy's hair. And not the Cassidy who spiked his milk with lemon juice for stealing her cookie the day before in the junior high lunchroom. And certainly not the

Cassidy who sat in the wreckage of that ill-fated prom table, golden eyes spitting fire even as tears dripped down red-stained cheeks.

This Cassidy possessed dignity, grace and strength wrapped in a package of vivid femininity. Any guy would be proud to have this woman walk beside him.

"Tim?" Her voice was soft…tentative. "Are you all right?"

He met her gaze and smiled. Slowly, shyly, a smile answered him.

"I think I'm in big trouble," he said. "If gaping at a beautiful woman was a crime, I'd be a lifer."

She laughed. He laughed. Dacy and Daria, the stinkers, exchanged high fives behind their cousin's back. But they probably deserved the mutual kudos if they'd had a hand in encouraging Cassidy to tread into territory that must number among her greatest fears.

He offered his arm. "Shall we?"

Cassidy stepped through the door and entrusted her hand to the crook of his elbow. "We shall." She glanced over her shoulder at the twins. "Don't wait up for us, kiddies."

The twins' laughter pealed as they poked their heads into the hallway.

"We're on your six, cuz," said one. "Our guys will be by to get us any second."

"Yeah, we've got your back," said the other.

Tim stopped and awarded them a long look. They sobered, meeting his gaze with wary intensity.

He lifted one corner of his mouth and inclined his head. "You may stand down for the evening, faithful watch-cousins. Cassidy is safe with me."

The twins exchanged glances.

"Am I nuts, sis?" said Dacy. "I think I believe him."

"I know. Right?" Daria answered.

A muffled snort from his companion alerted Tim to an impending unladylike guffaw. Swallowing his own chuckles, he hurried Cassidy around the corner. Others in formal attire were also gathering for a ride down to the banquet hall.

They joined the group and piled onto the elevator together. Cassidy finally released the amusement she'd been holding in. Tim followed suit. Every time they looked at each other, snickers claimed them. Their elevator companions started giving them the eye. Too bad. Tim vented another string of chuckles. This golden moment of innocent fun was too cleansing. Too enjoyable. Too right.

As they entered the banquet hall, he grabbed Cassidy's hand and squeezed. She squeezed back. This *was* going to be an awesome evening for the memory book, one he would treasure in years to come, even after the two of them inevitably went their separate ways. After all, a Halstead and a Ferris having a future together? Absurd. Her family would never accept him.

The room glittered with crystal and silver from the brightly lit chandeliers to the goblets and dinnerware on the elegantly set tables to the waitstaff bustling everywhere in dove-gray uniform jackets with silvery satin lapels. A string quartet played soft dinner music from a discreet corner. Savory smells teased the air from the mouthwatering dinner ready to be served.

A greeter escorted them to their designated table. Tim scanned the place tags and did a mental fist pump. Dacy and Daria had been assigned elsewhere. He wanted no competition for Cassidy's attention.

As Tim seated her, his hand brushed the side of her neck, and a tingle energized every pore. Did he imagine it, or had she shivered at the touch? He took his seat and met her gaze—solemn now, her eyes deep pools of amber.

"I'm thankful we've been given this opportunity to mend matters between us," she said.

"Me, too."

A soft silence fell between them, neither looking away. Their faces drew closer. Tim's heart performed the cha-cha against his ribs. He wanted to kiss her…right here…right now.

"Excuse me, sir," said a nasally voice.

Tim jerked back and looked up. A red-haired waiter with a goatee and dark-rimmed glasses stood behind them, presenting their salad plates. He placed the salads in front of them and withdrew as suddenly as he'd appeared. A soft giggle came from Cassidy. Tim forced a smile. If ever he'd pay to kick someone in the rear, this was the moment.

The meal passed in a clatter of fine silver against delicate china and exclamations of appreciation for the food. Their tablemates proved friendly and fun. Tim relaxed and abandoned his momentary irritation. Cassidy's laughter rang out often. She was enjoying herself. What more could he ask? Well, other than that kiss he meant to collect later on—a bittersweet memento.

The desserts arrived, the lights dimmed and Mindy stepped onto the stage to introduce the comedienne who had been booked for the evening. As she spoke, Tim settled back in his chair. Cassidy gazed over at him and smiled, and—

The microphone went dead as the room plunged into blackness. A universal gasp swept through the guests.

"Please remain in your seats, folks." Mindy's unamplified shout echoed across the room. "I'm sure it's the ice storm messing with our power. Our generator will kick in momentarily."

The roar of startled conversation settled into a dull rumble.

"What next?" Tim chuckled as he slid his arm across the back of Cassidy's chair.

Loose strands from her updo tickled the back of his hand. His fingers itched to tangle in the thick mass and draw her closer. *Easy does it, buddy.*

She leaned toward him, and her fragrance—jasmine with a kick of spice—wafted to him.

A ringtone sounded from the sequined handbag on her lap. "Oh, bother." She pulled out the phone, and the lit face revealed tension in the thinning of her lips. "I have to take this."

"Problem?"

"Answers. I hope. It's my partner calling from the precinct station." She rose.

Tim stood beside her.

"Stay here." Cassidy waved him down. "I'll pursue this conversation in the ladies' room, where it will be quieter. Don't worry. The light from my phone will guide my way." She glided away between the tables and was soon lost to view, except for the fading glow of her cell.

Independent female! Didn't give a guy a chance to tag along. Tim frowned. He couldn't exactly follow her into the ladies' room, but that didn't mean he had to let her get there alone—whether she wanted the escort or not.

Tim pulled his cell from his suit pocket, activated flashlight mode and let the beam guide him toward the door of the banquet hall. Stepping into the passageway, he looked to the left and then to the right. One direction led into the main lobby, which featured a set of restrooms, and the other direction led to a series of smaller meeting rooms, as well as another set of restrooms.

Which direction should he go? He chose left toward the meeting rooms and the lesser-used restrooms. Cassidy would want as much privacy as possible for her official conversation. Tim reached the restrooms without encountering her. He looked around. No one loitered nearby. Silence appeared to reign inside the ladies' room.

Okay, so tailing Cassidy hadn't been the best-thought-out endeavor of his life, but a nameless urgency wouldn't let him return to his seat. Face heating, Tim stuck his ear against the door. A slight sound of water running rewarded him. The sound abruptly ceased, and Tim stepped back just in time to avoid being caught eavesdropping by the woman who stepped out.

Not Cassidy.

"Is anyone else in there?" he asked.

In the muted glow of cell phone flashlights, Tim caught the startled-rabbit look the woman shot him. "Who wants to know?" She edged past him and scissor-stepped toward the safety of the group.

"So now I scared the daylights out of some

stranger," he muttered to himself. "Cassidy, I hope that phone call is solid gold." Tim sighed and shoved the restroom door open a few inches. No flashlight glow. "Anyone in here?" No answer.

She must have gone the other direction. Leave it to him to guess wrong about Cassidy Ferris.

A few minutes later, he'd investigated the other restroom by asking a few women if Cassidy was in there. They responded in the negative. The panic button in his gut pulsed on high alert.

In the middle of the lobby, Tim halted and dragged in several deep breaths. Where was the promised generator power? Had something other than an ice storm caused the loss of electricity? Was the *something* actually *someone* who had arranged this circumstance in order to do Cassidy harm? Snapshots flipped through his mind's eye—finding her crumpled against that aspen on the ski run, that car bearing down on her in the street, and then that chunk of ice rolling toward her head.

What if someone other than Jason Clement wanted her dead? What if the concierge had been a tool in the hands of a more devious killer? What if Cassidy had already become his victim?

God? Help!

EIGHT

Cassidy floated toward consciousness. If common sense didn't assure her that her head was still attached to her body, she wouldn't know it for any feeling below her neck, though she did sense that her arms were stretched over her head.

Silence enshrouded her. Did darkness, too?

She forced her eyes open, but her lids only cooperated sufficiently to form slits. Evidently she lay flat on her back, because a ceiling hovered above her, bathed in a flickering glow. Clearly, electrical power had not yet returned to the building.

Had the staff brought candles or oil lamps into the banquet hall? No, the ceiling was too close. This couldn't be the banquet area. Had she fainted and been carried someplace to recover? Not hardly! Cassidy Ferris never fainted. Maybe she tripped over her gown's hem and hit her head. That idea made better sense, except for the lack of throbbing in her skull. Unless her hearing was as impaired as her sense of touch, she was alone here—wherever here was.

The last thing Cassidy remembered was her cell phone ringing. After that, everything was blank.

A soft hum carried to her. The silhouette of someone sitting in a small motorized chair took shape. The person guided his chair closer. The skin of Cassidy's scalp tingled, and her heart pounded. Whoever approached might not mean her well, and she was helpless to defend herself.

An ever-present help in time of trouble...

The fragment of a Bible verse she'd learned in Sunday school flowed through her mind. *Okay, God. I'm in Your hands.*

The person stopped mere feet from her. The chair was mostly obscured below where Cassidy lay. However, the torso—but not the features of the face—had grown clearer. A man gazed upon her from his motorized throne. She must be lying on something raised above the floor. A bed perhaps?

"Feeling better, girlie?" said a voice that sounded as if sandpaper had roughed up the vocal cords.

Cassidy swallowed against a dry throat. Should she pretend unconsciousness?

The man shook her arm. What do you know? Sensation! The hand that touched her must have been abraded by the same sandpaper that messed up his vocal cords—either that or this person was part scaly fish. Her skin crawled.

"You need to wake up and get out of here," the man told her. "They'll be back any minute."

Okay, wheelchair guy might not be a bad person—at least not the main one.

"I'm coming around," she said, her voice a faint whisper. "Still can't move."

"Wish you could stay," he said. "Don't get visitors much. They guard me round the clock."

Why was this guy under watch? Was he an unstable lunatic? He wasn't quite all there, that was for sure. And, yet, the wistfulness of his tone conveyed not threat but pouty sadness.

The man leaned toward her, and the glow of a candle flickering near her head illuminated grotesquely marred facial features that seemed somehow vaguely familiar. Something flashed, and a knife in an equally marred hand streaked toward her.

Cassidy screamed.

Urgent voices drew Tim's attention. A maintenance technician and Mindy-the-Manager entered the lobby, pushing carts loaded with what looked like oil lanterns, candles and flashlights. Apparently, the power wasn't going to be restored soon. Tim caught the words "send someone upstairs to get the new owner's authorization" from the technician and "not to be disturbed under any circumstances" from the manager.

Who was not to be disturbed? The new owner? Was he or she in the building? Why couldn't the person be bothered in a crisis like this?

Tim stepped into the path of the bickering pair, and they halted abruptly.

"Excuse me, sir." Mindy's tone was frayed around the edges. "Please take one of these," she held out a flashlight, "and return to your seat in the banquet hall until we get things sorted out so people can move around safely."

"Things?" Tim said. "You mean like repairing or replacing the generator?"

"Replacing," the technician burst out with force. "It's junk and I—"

He stopped speaking, mouth agape. Had Mindy delivered a sly kick?

"Get your cartload to the rest of the staff for distribution," she said, and the technician moved off, grumbling under his breath.

She turned toward Tim. "We will manage until the power company can repair the lines. The staff is organizing games and activities that can be played by flashlight or lamplight. The evening will still be fun."

"Not unless I can locate the woman who was with me," Tim said. "She's disappeared."

"Perhaps she returned to her room." The sugary tone oozed sympathy for a ditched date.

Tim opened his mouth but words didn't emerge.

Had Cassidy grown bored with the evening and blown him off? Such meanness didn't ring true to her character. But maybe something in that phone call sent her someplace in the facility to investigate. Excluding him from cop business made sense, but did nothing to reassure him she wasn't in trouble.

Where should he start looking? The odd reference to the lodge's owner bugged him. It might be nothing, but it could be something.

"I overheard mention of a new owner," he said. "Who is it?"

Several beats of silence answered him then Mindy sighed. "I really do need to attend to my other guests, sir, but it can't hurt to tell you that we've been acquired by Halstead Enterprises."

A polar-plunge sensation engulfed Tim. His father's company owned the lodge?

"Dad is *here?*" The words escaped from him more as an outburst of personal revelation than a true question.

Mindy took a step backward. "Then you *are* a member of *that* Halstead family. I wasn't sure and I didn't want to assume."

"Where is he?"

The edge in Tim's tone sent her back another step. "I don't want to get involved in family politics. Besides, you really mustn't disturb him. He's not a well man."

"All the more reason that I need to see my father. You can either tell me where he is, or I will disturb every guest in the place until I find him." And hopefully Cassidy, too.

Mindy stuttered out the location, and Tim took off for the stairwell. His family had a suite reserved on the third floor at the far end of the west wing. Windows looking out into the courtyard from there would have offered a prime location from which to blast off the head of that ice sculpture with a silenced rifle. But why would his dad want to kill Cassidy? And why arrange for his son to witness the tragedy?

Or maybe Dad wanted them both dead. In their own ways, Cassidy and he were thorns in the side of Halstead Enterprises. The senior Halstead was prone to paying for favors under the table and twisting the rules through legal chicanery, but murder had never been his style in dealing with enemies.

Or had it?

Tim halted his ascent on the landing outside the third-floor hallway. In hindsight, it was odd how many times some form of disaster befell human obstructions in the path of Halstead Enterprises. More than coincidence? Time to find out.

Steeling his jaw, Tim grasped the door handle, pulled it open and pointed the beam of his cell light into the hallway. Directly before him loomed the door displaying the number of his father's suite. Lacking the means to pull off a sneak approach, Tim took the only action available to him. He knocked.

A gravelly yelp carried to him from within. He stuck his ear to the door panel. Did a female voice say something? Cassidy?

It had been a long time since his football days, but he'd managed a decent tackle today. Maybe he was up for smashing down a door.

He took a step backward, and something cold and hard pressed against the back of his neck. The distinctive click of a cocking pistol froze him in place.

"You took your sweet time figuring it out and accepting the invitation," said a smooth, familiar voice. "Welcome to the liveliest New Year's Eve party in the lodge. I promise you, it's to die for."

Cassidy sat on the edge of the bed, commanding her legs to operate. The disfigured man had cut her arms loose from the headboard, and she'd been working hard the last few minutes to reclaim the use of her limbs from the grip of whatever drug she'd been given. Now someone was at the door, and her odd ally had yelped and powered himself out of the room.

"It can't be whoever is holding you prisoner here," she called to him. "They would have a key."

Then who was it? Room service?

Cassidy tried again to stand and achieved a se-microuch, muscles quivering. But then her legs gave out, and she plopped down on the edge of the bed. She ground her teeth together. Talk about living her greatest nightmare! She was helpless in the face of evil. If she got out of this, it wouldn't be by her own efforts.

Okay, God. I hear You. I get it. Help!

In the outer room, a door opened. Cassidy's skin prickled.

"That's it. Go right in." The unfamiliar voice was bathed in mockery.

Who was entering? More than one person, apparently.

"Where's Cassidy?" spoke a second voice.

Tim!

"I'm here," she called.

The knowledge of his presence spurted strength through her, and she rose. On tottery legs, she made it to the doorway and leaned against the frame.

Someone in shadows stood with one arm stretched toward Tim. The man's hand probably held a gun, though she couldn't make out the weapon. The person edged toward an oil lamp on a side table and turned up the light. Seeing the guy's face didn't help her identify him. He was middle-aged, short and plump with craggy features and a thick shock of gray hair, and wore a long-sleeve business shirt and sharply creased slacks. The object in his hand was a Glock pistol with a silencer attached. Death on a hair trigger. No surprises there. She'd give long odds that a silenced rifle was somewhere in the suite, as well.

"Cass." Tim breathed her name as if it were a treasure.

Their gazes met, and a shock of warmth flooded through her. *I love him.* The words seared her brain. *I have for a long time. Why didn't I know sooner?*

Her legs weakened, and she clutched the door post.

"You'd better sit down before you fall down," the stranger said. "The benzo in your soft drink can't have worn off completely. I'm surprised you're moving. Hard to know how much to give a gal your size."

He turned his head toward the man in the wheelchair. The invalid had parked himself in deep shadow and sat hunched as if he could make himself small enough not to be noticed.

The gunman clucked his tongue. "You cut her loose. Naughty-naughty."

Tim put an arm around Cassidy's waist. She leaned into him as he guided her toward a small settee. If this was the last embrace from him that she would experience in this life, she meant to savor it.

"You sit, too," the gunman barked at Tim.

He settled beside Cassidy and took her hand in his.

"Who is our uncordial host?" she asked.

"Meet Glen Reece, my father's personal assistant." Tim glared up at the man with the gun. "Where's Dad, and who else are you holding hostage here?" He waved toward the man in the wheelchair.

Glen chuckled. Not a nice sound. "Come on out." He motioned with the barrel of the gun. "Here's the one you've been sniveling for months to see."

With a motorized hum, the wheelchair glided into the lamplight. The occupant lifted his scarred chin and did his best to square twisted shoulders and pull himself into a straight posture. The effort highlighted the pitiful remnants of what must once have been a tall, sturdy physique.

A bolt of recognition flashed through Cassidy, even as Tim gasped and lunged forward. He knelt in front of the wheelchair and clasped a scarred paw between his hands.

"Dad! What happened? No, never mind. The accident last year. Glen lied to me that you were all right and didn't want to see me."

A sob wrenched the senior Halstead's chest. "I've needed you to come—"

The door flew open and clipped the tail from Thomas Halstead's sentence.

Cassidy whipped her gaze toward the suite entrance and gaped at the person who stepped inside. Could this whole evening get any stranger?

Tim narrowed his eyes at the intruder. The annoying redheaded waiter from the banquet. The one who served them all evening. What was he doing here? Check that. No matter.

"Run!" he cried. "Go call the police."

The waiter shut the door. "I don't think I'll do that, bro."

No more nasally whine. This voice was well-known, and once upon a time well loved. Tim's heart stalled.

"Funny how the smallest changes in appearance can disguise a person." Trace pulled the glasses from his nose and the red wig off his head, revealing thick, blond hair similar to Tim's, only cut shorter. "You had no idea who I was until this moment." His laugh turned into a wince as he yanked the goatee from his chin.

Tim rose to his feet and glared at his sibling.

"You've been trying to kill Cassidy. And, I think, me, too."

"*Trying* is the operative word. I caught wind

that the Giraffe was trying to long-neck into my private enterprise. If Clement had been a more capable assassin, she'd be toast by now, and I would have had a great laugh about the irony of forcing you to witness the unfortunate demise of your secret crush."

"My crush?" Tim gaped.

Trace rolled his eyes. "You and she may be the only ones on the planet who can't see the hot vibes between you two."

Tim clamped his jaw shut. What he felt for Cassidy might have been described as an inside-out crush back in their high school days. Now it was much more, but he was in no position to say so.

"With Cassidy out of the way," his brother continued, "that would have left only you and dear old Dad to deal with. But I ended up needing to take the useless dweeb out of the picture before his clumsy attempts exposed us all."

"So you *murdered* the concierge?" Cassidy said, voice hard.

"Sharp as always." Trace delivered a mock bow. "Don't you look stunning. I had no idea you cleaned up so nicely. I wasn't inclined to notice while Glen and I sweated through hauling your limp form up the stairs. Toting a six-foot-plus woman is no picnic."

Cassidy scowled. "I'm delighted to have caused you trouble."

Tim stepped forward. "What's your game, Trace?"

His brother shrugged. "You may as well get the scoop before Glen and I set up the scene that will solve all my problems. As you can see—" he waved toward his father "—Dad was badly hurt in the accident in Rio. Medical staff recommended that I pull the plug, but I refused for one reason—the old man had been dragging his feet about cutting you out of his will. Thinking you'd come to your senses and return to the fold. But I couldn't chance a goody-goody wimp inheriting any interest in Halstead Enterprises. So I needed to keep the extent of Dad's injuries a secret and make sure he lived long enough to sign a new will."

A whine rasped from his father's throat. "I'm not signing anything, no matter how mean you are to me."

"You don't have to worry about that anymore, Dad." Trace grinned. "I'm done waiting for your stubbornness to run out. You're about to gun down your turncoat son, and when Cassidy tries to stop you, she bites the dust, too. The stress is too much for your heart, and you expire on the spot—with a little help from a special medication, undetectable on autopsy." He patted his shirt pocket. "Tim might still be in the will, but he'll no longer be alive to collect. Just me."

"And me," Glen put in. "Don't forget our agreement. A third interest in the company."

Trace glowered. "Only *after* I'm in control can that be arranged. *I'm* your bread and butter."

"Let's get to it then."

"Wait just a rotten second," Cassidy burst out. "I want to know one more thing."

"What's that?" Trace sneered.

"Did you have anything to do with Francine's death?"

Trace rolled back on his heels. If Tim wasn't mistaken, the question dealt his brother a verbal right hook. What role *had* his brother played?

"Where did you come up with that question?" Trace snapped.

"Just this weekend," Cassidy said, "the twins and I figured out Francine's part in the shove that landed me in the punch at prom. Shortly before Francine died, she made a strange comment to Dacy. Something about the mistake costing her soul. What did she mean? I think you have an answer."

"Ever the clever detective." He lifted his hands in mock surrender, but Tim knew his brother too well not to note the tick in the corner of his left eye that betrayed an explosion simmering to happen. "I was the only eyewitness to her tripping Tim and used the information to my advantage. She did a few…uh…minor business errands. Nothing major. Didn't even know what she was doing at first. An ideal mule. Nobody would suspect a straight-ace Ferris."

Tim made impotent fists. "You blackmailed her because she couldn't bear to have her cousins know about tripping me!"

"Don't go all self-righteous on me, brother. Back then, you might have seized the same advantage."

"I don't think so."

Cassidy brushed Tim's hand with the tips of her fingers. She must be regaining some muscle control. Their gazes locked.

"You would never have resorted to blackmail," she said. "Or dealt drugs—then or now."

Tim's heart melted in the heat of her fervent faith in him. She believed in him, even when the issue went back to his wild days.

She pointed a glare at Trace. "Tim and I picked on each other fiercely, but I never saw him bully or exploit a weaker person. Frani was insecure and vulnerable from her family's predicament. Guilt from knuckling under you probably drove her to take the Valium that locked her in a deep sleep in spite of the fire alarm."

Tim jerked. "Francine was drugged that night? I didn't know."

Cassidy hung her head. "Our family asked the

authorities to keep that detail quiet. We couldn't bear to add insult to tragedy."

"You might as well know the story." Trace's laugh held a jagged edge. "Lovely Frani was going to turn me in, regardless of personal consequences. She told me so when we met in the basement of her apartment complex the night of the fire. I couldn't let a snitch put an end to a prosperous business. It wasn't hard to drop a generous dose into the Coke she had with her, wait a little while for it to take effect, and then short out the electrical box. Looks like a tragic accident, and—poof!—a problem goes away."

Dad released a deep-throated gurgle. "What sort of monster did I raise?"

"You're the monster, you disgusting waste of breath." Spewing curses, Trace charged for their father.

Tim stepped between them even as Cassidy surged from the settee and rammed Glen in the gut. The gun roared, but Tim's view of events was lost as offensive tackle and linebacker collided. He and his brother hit the floor, rolling, punching, no holds barred.

They used to tangle like this when they were kids, but in roughhouse play. This was deadly business. All hot breath and grunts of pain and effort. If he lived, he'd be black-and-blue tomorrow.

If. At any moment, Glen could put a bullet into him. He had to win, and win fast, to help Cassidy.

They rolled again, putting Trace on top. Tim bucked and threw a left at his brother's chin. His fist connected even as a crash sent shards of ceramic spraying in every direction. Trace went limp and flopped onto his side. Tim gazed up at his father in the wheelchair, staring down at him, teary-eyed, the remnants of a lamp in one gnarled fist.

"Cassidy!"

Tim bounded to his feet, searching the room for her and Glen. There. She stood over a prone but conscious and groaning Glen, holding his pistol on him.

She grinned. "Nice work, Halstead. Or should I say Halsteads?"

Tim melted to his knees. He loved Cassidy Ferris. Couldn't imagine a world without her. But after the horror of his brother's confession, he couldn't imagine a world in which they could be together. Francine's innocent blood would always stand between them.

NINE

Three months later

"Somebody give me CPR! Tim Halstead has moved home." Daria tapped the daily newspaper she was browsing through in the family room of Cassidy's parents' house.

"Get outta here!" Dacy trotted across the room to look over her sister's shoulder.

"Don't tease," Cassidy snapped.

The extended tribe was gathered for the monthly Ferris family supper. A hubbub of voices and laughter, as well as savory cooking smells, filled every crevice of the split-level home. Stretched out on an easy chair amid an assortment of cousins, nieces, nephews, aunts and uncles, Cassidy picked at a hangnail. How soon could she graciously depart the festivities? Or maybe she should retreat to the privacy of her old bedroom until she had to emerge and fill a chair at the table. What a wet blanket she was these days. She had to snap out of it.

"No, look, Cass." Daria brought the paper to her. "This article says Tim has taken over the family business."

"What?" Electrified, Cassidy sat up. The rat! At the first opportunity he betrayed the compassionate values he'd spouted over New Year's weekend. Stomach twisting, she looked down at the headline on the business news page.

Halstead Son to Redirect Halstead Enterprises

Redirect? That sounded positive. Cassidy dove in and absorbed the article. Tim had indeed moved home to Seattle and taken over the leadership of Halstead Enterprises. His future plans included upgrades and renovations to existing apartment complexes across the West Coast, as well as possible new construction.

One quotation from him said, "We want to offer decent dwellings for those struggling with the adversities life can generously dish out."

Cassidy stifled a laugh. Typical Tim-ese with the lofty language. But she heard his heart, and it was beautiful. Her own had begun to thud like a bongo drum. What was the matter with her?

They'd gone their separate ways after that chaotic weekend. No doubt they'd see each other again at the trial of Trace Halstead, where they would both need to testify. How painful for Tim! Glen

Reece, the creepy-crawler, had worked a plea deal with the DA and would also testify against Trace.

"Call him." The voice was her mother's.

Cassidy looked up to find her older and wiser—albeit significantly shorter—mirror image, holding out the handset from the cordless phone and a phone book opened to the page listing the Thomas Halstead residence.

"Me, call?" Was that *her* voice squeaking like a rusty hinge?

"You devoured the news story, grinning like the Cheshire cat's first cousin, when you've hardly cracked a smile since you returned from Aspen. We've been giving you space, thinking you needed time to recover from the trauma of the murder attempts and the revelations that have rocked all our worlds, but now I see a bigger picture. You like that young man—maybe more than like—and his sense of family guilt will probably keep him from picking up the phone. Yes, my gutsy daughter, you should call him." She waggled the phone.

As if moving through sludge, Cassidy accepted the phone and the book. Did anyone notice the tremor in her hands? Silence had fallen, and expectant faces focused on her from every angle of the room.

"Can't a girl have a little privacy to make a phone call?" She scowled ferociously.

Laughing and hooting, the family mob departed

as if a vacuum had sucked them from the room. The same vacuum seemed to have stolen the air from Cassidy's lungs.

Come on, Detective Ferris. If you can face down a tweeker, you can talk to Tim.

Sure. No problem. She'd call him about the article. Congratulate him. Inquire about his father. They could have a polite conversation, and then… What if he didn't say he wanted to see her again? Her heart would shatter into tiny pieces.

Her lips trembled. Was she willing to take that chance?

Hearing his father's gravelly chuckle and one side of a conversation, Tim headed for the foyer. Who could be chatting up his dad on the phone?

Frowning, he scanned the marble-and-hardwood environment he'd once taken for granted. This place had to go. He had nothing against people having nice things—he liked them as well as anyone—but the mammoth house had been built and maintained by the sweat and tears of the down-and-out. His new business approach would necessitate stripping the family assets to the bare bones for the capital to pull it off. They would come back, of course, but in a manner that restored respect to the Halstead name and honored God.

"Here he is," his dad said.

Smirking, fit to puff up and float out of his chair, Dad extended the handset.

"For me?"

"Unless the Invisible Man is standing beside you."

Gingerly, Tim accepted the phone. Cackling, his father powered his chair toward the dining room. From the scents wafting to Tim's nose, their cook had supper nearly ready to serve. Too bad his appetite hadn't picked up since the night of the New Year's Eve banquet.

"Hello?"

"Um, hi…It's Cassidy—er, Cass."

Something like fireworks went off in Tim's chest. Cass? No, this had to be some joke. The Cassidy he knew never sounded timid.

"I read the article in the newspaper." The voice gathered steam, sounding a little more like Cassidy. "I'm impressed with the new direction you're taking the company. Congratulations!"

A smile bobbled on the edges of Tim's lips. She was reaching out to him, but was she merely being polite?

"Thanks. I appreciate the encouragement. It's going to be a tough road for a while, but I believe the results will be worth the struggle."

"I do, too."

A few beats of silence dangled between them.

"Your dad sounds like he's doing well," she said.

"Are you doing all right?" he said.

Their words had tumbled out simultaneously, and they laughed. Tension ebbed, and Tim perched a hip on the edge of the table. He was up for a chat as long as she wanted to stay on the line.

"My dad has his good days and his bad days," he said. "But he tells me he has good days more often since I've been in charge of his care."

"I don't find that hard to believe. What's his prognosis?"

"The accident did a number on him. Not just physically. As you experienced, he can still be sly and sneaky, but he's no longer ruthless…or particularly greedy—except for love and attention. His mind is…more simple than it used to be, and the medical professionals don't know when or if that will change. They think it's amazing he has so much of his faculties left. How about you? Things getting back to normal?"

"Normal? What's that?" She laughed, but there was a roughness to the sound.

"Give yourself time to find new equilibrium. The things Trace revealed are hard to take."

"That's not it."

"What then?"

"I…miss you."

Tim's pulse went bonkers. She missed him!

"I more than miss you." His voice was suddenly

thick. "But I can't expect your family to accept me after—"

"Let me talk to the guy," intruded a male voice on her end.

Silence fell, except for a muted whispery sound, as if she'd covered the receiver with her hand and was conducting a hissed conversation with someone.

"My uncle wants to speak to you." She finally came back on. Her tone was strained. "Francine's father."

Tim's gut went hollow, but he might as well take it over the phone than somewhere the guy could get arrested for assaulting him. "Put him on."

"Gus Ferris, here," a strong baritone spoke. "Short for Augustus, but if you ever call me that I'll have to whip the nonsense out of you, young man."

Tim went very still on the inside. Did that statement imply an offer to get to know him?

"My wife and I have done a lot of soul-searching since the full truth came out," Gus went on. "In a way, it's a great relief to understand that our daughter did not willingly take drugs. But in another way, it changes nothing. Frani is gone, and her mom and I still occasionally fight the temptation to beat ourselves up that we were both working the night of the fire. Had we been there, we could have carried her to safety. We can't change any of that, but here's what we can change—our attitude."

The man inhaled a long, audible breath. "You are innocent of anything to do with our daughter's death, plus you saved my niece's life. Now I hear you've grown up into a decent Christian fellow. Only one thing remains against you."

Tim cleared thickness from his throat. "What's that, sir?"

"Gus. I told you, it's Gus. Now why don't you ask Cassidy out? I'm tired of her mooning around."

"I don't moon!" came an indistinct yell.

"Like a calf, you don't!" To Cassidy. "What do you say, Tim? Want to join us for a Ferris family supper?"

"When?" Tim's heart started trying to kangaroo-hop out of his chest.

"Does right now work?"

"I was about to sit down to eat with my father. How about—"

"If you go out, can I have my supper in front of the television?" Dad interrupted from the dining room doorway.

Tim lowered the receiver and cocked a brow at his father. The boyish grin on the man's scarred face released Tim from any guilt about missing a meal with him.

"This once," he said.

Dad performed a fist-pump.

Grinning, Tim restored the receiver to his lips. "I'll be right over."

* * * * *

Dear Reader,

Whew! That was close! I'm so glad Cassidy and Tim came out of this adventure alive and in love. Aren't you?

I so enjoyed writing about these beloved enemies. Did you have a high school (or elementary school) nemesis? Were you someone's nemesis? If so, I hope this tale of the rocky road to love and forgiveness inspires you to make it right—if only in your own heart between you and God.

The Lord charges us many times in scripture to uphold the rights of the poor and oppressed, and warns sternly about becoming one of the oppressors. To their mutual surprise, Cassidy's crusading personality and Tim's humbly passionate conviction click to make them an effective team. My prayer is for the Lord to bring such teammates into the lives of all my readers, so our usefulness in the Kingdom of God may be enhanced.

In case you haven't noticed, I write what I like to read—tales of adventure seasoned with romance, humor and faith. Drop in and visit me on the web at www.jillelizabethnelson.com or you can look me up on Facebook at www.facebook.com/JillElizabethNelson.Author.

Abundant Blessings,
Jill Elizabeth Nelson

Questions for Discussion

1. Cassidy and Tim have a negative history that has colored their lives into their present. Do you have any people in your life who once were your enemies, but now are your friends? How did that come about? Was it a God thing?

2. Cassidy has a view of herself that isn't positive in certain areas. Is her opinion accurate? Why or why not?

3. Tim resolves to protect Cassidy by way of atonement for his family's sins against hers. Are there times in your life when you've made irrational resolutions out of feelings of guilt? How effective were those resolutions?

4. Cassidy has grown up under the microscope of a large and tight-knit extended family. What effect has this environment had on the way she perceives herself and the way she interacts with Tim? What are the advantages or disadvantages of this type of family unit?

5. Though Francine never appears live on the stage of this story, her life and death have profoundly impacted every main character. Discuss that impact on Cassidy, Tim, Dacy, Daria

and Trace individually and on the way they interact with one another. How deeply do gone-but-not-forgotten people affect your own life?

LARGER-PRINT BOOKS!

GET 2 FREE LARGER-PRINT NOVELS PLUS 2 FREE MYSTERY GIFTS

Love Inspired®

SUSPENSE
RIVETING INSPIRATIONAL ROMANCE

Larger-print novels are now available...

YES! Please send me 2 FREE LARGER-PRINT Love Inspired® Suspense novels and my 2 FREE mystery gifts (gifts are worth about $10). After receiving them, if I don't wish to receive any more books, I can return the shipping statement marked "cancel." If I don't cancel, I will receive 4 brand-new novels every month and be billed just $5.24 per book in the U.S. or $5.74 per book in Canada. That's a savings of at least 23% off the cover price. It's quite a bargain! Shipping and handling is just 50¢ per book in the U.S. and 75¢ per book in Canada.* I understand that accepting the 2 free books and gifts places me under no obligation to buy anything. I can always return a shipment and cancel at any time. Even if I never buy another book, the two free books and gifts are mine to keep forever.

110/310 IDN F5AY

Name	(PLEASE PRINT)

Address	Apt. #

City	State/Prov.	Zip/Postal Code

Signature (if under 18, a parent or guardian must sign)

Mail to the Harlequin® Reader Service:
IN U.S.A.: P.O. Box 1867, Buffalo, NY 14240-1867
IN CANADA: P.O. Box 609, Fort Erie, Ontario L2A 5X3

**Are you a current subscriber to Love Inspired Suspense books and want to receive the larger-print edition?
Call 1-800-873-8635 or visit www.ReaderService.com.**

* Terms and prices subject to change without notice. Prices do not include applicable taxes. Sales tax applicable in N.Y. Canadian residents will be charged applicable taxes. Offer not valid in Quebec. This offer is limited to one order per household. Not valid for current subscribers to Love Inspired Suspense larger-print books. All orders subject to credit approval. Credit or debit balances in a customer's account(s) may be offset by any other outstanding balance owed by or to the customer. Please allow 4 to 6 weeks for delivery. Offer available while quantities last.

Your Privacy—The Harlequin® Reader Service is committed to protecting your privacy. Our Privacy Policy is available online at www.ReaderService.com or upon request from the Harlequin Reader Service.

We make a portion of our mailing list available to reputable third parties that offer products we believe may interest you. If you prefer that we not exchange your name with third parties, or if you wish to clarify or modify your communication preferences, please visit us at www.ReaderService.com/consumerchoice or write to us at Harlequin Reader Service Preference Service, P.O. Box 9062, Buffalo, NY 14269. Include your complete name and address.

LISLP13R